He cleared his throat, but he still could hardly speak.

"Thanks for dinner."

Very slowly, she raised her hand until she loosely wrapped her fingers around his wrist. Her voice came out lower in pitch than usual, almost husky. "You're welcome."

The silky sound made his heart race and her touch made his brain misfire. He reached up with his other hand until he cradled her cheeks in both hands. She still didn't move away, nor did she show any signs of hesitation.

"Sarah. . . ," he muttered as he lowered his head to hers, letting his voice trail off when his lips touched hers. Slowly and gently, he kissed her warm, soft lips. She lifted her head just a little within the cradle of his hands and returned his kiss.

Matt's heart kicked into overdrive. He wanted to slip his arms around her back and hold her tight and kiss her well and good, but this wasn't the right time for that. Using all the self-control he could muster, he pulled back and let his arms fall to his sides. "Bye, Sarah. I guess I'll see you around."

Before she could tell him that wasn't such a good idea, he turned, opened the door, and left.

GAIL SATTLER lives in Vancouver, BC (where you don't have to shovel rain) with her husband, three sons, two dogs, five lizards, and countless fish, many of whom have names. She writes inspirational romance because she loves happily-ever-afters and believes God has a place in that happy ending. Visit Gail's website at www.gailsattler.com.

Books by Gail Sattler
HEARTSONG PRESENTS

HP269—Walking the Dog	HP433—A Few Flowers
HP306—Piano Lessons	HP445—McMillian's
HP325—Gone Camping	Matchmakers
HP358—At Arm's Length	HP464—The Train Stops Here
HP385—On the Road Again	HP473—The Wedding's On
HP397—My Name Is Mike	HP509—His Christmas Angel
HP406—Almost Twins	HP530—Joe's Diner

A note from the Author:
I love to hear from my readers! You may correspond with me by writing:

> **Gail Sattler**
> **Author Relations**
> **PO Box 719**
> **Uhrichsville, OH 44683**

Don't miss out on any of our super romances. Write to us at the following address for information on our newest releases and club information.

Heartsong Presents Readers' Service
PO Box 721
Uhrichsville, OH 44683

Or check out our website at www.heartsongpresents.com

A Donut a Day

Gail Sattler

Heartsong Presents

Dedicated to Royal Canadian Mounted Police Constable Lloyd Bigelow and Retired Corporal Bev Dodd. Words cannot convey my thanks for the time and energy you spent with me and all my questions. Special mention goes to every member of every police force, everywhere. You are all heroes; you make the world a safer place. God bless you all!

GLOSSARY OF TERMS

RCMP =ROYAL CANADIAN MOUNTED POLICE
ETA = ESTIMATED TIME OF ARRIVAL
MVA = MOTOR VEHICLE ACCIDENT
BOLF = BE ON THE LOOKOUT FOR
NCO = NONCOMMISSIONED OFFICER, CAN BE THE RANK OF CORPORAL, SERGEANT, STAFF SERGEANT
GIS = GENERAL INVESTIGATION SECTION AKA (ALSO KNOWN AS) PLAIN CLOTHES SECTION

ISBN 1-58660-865-7

A DONUT A DAY

one

Matt pulled the squad car into the parking lot of Donnie's Donuts. He punched a ten-seven into the mobile computer and typed the address to tell the dispatcher his location. He shut off the car and, out of habit, exited quickly.

While Ty pulled up beside him and followed the same procedure, Matt clicked his portable radio to make sure it was on. "How much time do you think we'll get tonight?" he mumbled as Ty got out of his squad car.

Ty checked his wristwatch and his own portable radio. "Don't know. I've needed this break for hours."

Matt let out a long sigh. "Me too," he muttered.

After two motor vehicle accidents, one with a fatality, he'd arrived too late at a robbery to do any more than ask questions. Next, he'd been called to break up a rowdy party, even though he knew everything would resume within minutes after he left. He looked down at the Royal Canadian Mounted Police logo on his car door. Someone had hit his car with an egg while he was at the door of the house.

His last call, a domestic, had been the most difficult. When he and the other officer arrived, the woman, her nose still bleeding and tears streaming down her bruised face, claimed she fell. She wouldn't press charges. As he made his report on any domestic, he always took a few minutes to pray for the people involved. He knew he was supposed to distance himself, but sometimes he couldn't. At least this time he had arrived before one of the people involved required hospitalization—or worse.

Even though he knew he would lie awake for hours after what he'd seen tonight, Matt just wanted to go home and go to bed. However, with nearly three more hours left in his shift, he could only take a break and hope he had time to eat before the next disaster struck.

Matt and Ty turned toward each other. Everything around them was peaceful and still. Even the normally busy street was quiet. Of course, it was 3:30 A.M. on a weeknight. The only people out at this hour were those working odd shifts, the drunks, the thieves, and the troublemakers.

After the night he'd had, the sudden quiet felt like being in the eye of a hurricane. He tried to shake the foreboding that, as soon as they sat down with their coffees, the radio would blast out some instructions, and they'd be in for more of the same. Unfortunately, this was too often the case. He didn't want today to be another one of those days.

"Let's go in now, while we still can."

The words were barely out of his mouth when a pickup truck whizzed down the main road at approximately thirty miles per hour over the posted speed limit.

Matt stiffened, his hand still on the button of his mobile radio. "Is it worth it?"

Ty shook his head. "The speed we'd have to go to catch up, if he doesn't turn, wouldn't be worth the risk just for a speeding ticket. I don't remember that kind of pickup on the BOLF list. Let's go in."

As they walked toward the building, Matt noted a semi, complete with a trailer, parked on the street, then checked out the parking lot. Besides two small cars parked in the corner, which he knew was the area designated for employees, and the two squad cars, the only other car was a familiar large late model with a bent antenna and a mismatched door.

"Guess who?" Ty mumbled.

"The Ronskys," Matt mumbled. "At least they're here and not out causing trouble." Matt pulled the glass door open and walked inside, speaking softly to Ty over his shoulder. "At least not yet."

Sure enough, the punks in question were holed up in the

corner table. Tonight all five of them were together, speaking loudly, every second word a colorful expletive. The trucker sat alone in the corner, reading a newspaper, a coffee mug and a half-eaten donut in front of him on the table.

Matt and Ty walked to the front counter without breaking stride.

"Good evening, gentlemen. What will it be today?" The woman's face changed from a polite welcoming smile to a full ear-to-ear grin. She looked Matt straight in the eye. "I'll bet this is a café mocha and cranberry muffin day for you, Constable Walker."

Matt broke into a smile, the first of his shift. Seeing Sarah was truly the only bright spot of the night.

Often when he entered an establishment, alone or with another member, people became tense or fidgety. Personally, he could never understand why anyone would be nervous of the police if they hadn't done anything wrong, but he saw it all the time.

Other people treated him with complete and utter disdain, as if he were the bad guy or seeking innocent people to harass. Nothing could be further from the truth.

Sometimes the late-night managers asked him to speak to rowdy patrons to either settle them or evict them from the premises. While it was his duty to keep peace and order, he also needed some time off while he could get it, before the next call came in. On the flip side, some late-night staff made it obvious they didn't want the RCMP to come in late at night because they made the rest of the clientele uncomfortable.

Sarah simply treated him like a man who needed a break after too many hours of hard and often emotionally draining work. Stopping at Donnie's Donuts was the breath of fresh air he needed when working a twelve-hour night shift, and seeing Sarah made it even better.

Sarah seemed to be about his age, maybe a little younger, in her late twenties. He supposed she wasn't bad looking, but he couldn't tell for sure. She always wore the same, shapeless blue uniform smock with the Donnie's Donuts logo. She never wore make-up, and she always wore her light brown hair pulled back in a stark, tight ponytail. He didn't know how long her hair was, because he'd never seen it down. Beyond her pleasant and welcoming smile, Sarah's best feature had to be her eyes. They were a unique sea green color, and they shone when she smiled.

"Hi, Sarah. That sounds great."

She nodded and immediately punched his order into the cash register. He didn't know how she did it, but most of the time Sarah seemed to be able to tell what kind of night he was having by looking at him. Sometimes he needed to listen to bright and inane conversation. Sometimes he wanted nothing more than to sit in silence and stare into the bottom of his cup. Somehow she usually matched his mood with the right kind of muffin or a donut. She even suggested different kinds of coffee for him—flavored coffees when he was having an easy day, stronger coffees when he felt tired, or sometimes, like today, something both strong and sweet when he needed a pick-me-up.

Not that Sarah talked to him much. They weren't on a first-name basis. She knew him as Constable Walker because his name tag displayed his rank, last name, and first initial. Matt knew her as Sarah because her nametag showed only her first name.

Sarah turned and smiled at Ty. "And for you, Constable Edwards, a vanilla latté and a chocolate chip muffin?"

Matt could almost see Ty drooling. "That sounds great, Sarah. Thanks."

Out of the corner of his eye, Matt saw the Ronsky clan and their accompanying entourage hustle out the door, leaving their unfinished coffees behind. Sarah sighed with relief but said nothing.

Ty excused himself, leaving Matt standing at the counter to pay. After Sarah accepted his money, she turned around to select the two muffins and prepare the two cups of specialty coffee. While she waited for the machine to do its work, Sarah positioned the fingers of her left hand into the shape of a guitar chord. In time to the music of one of the local radio stations drifting in from the speaker overhead, she strummed the air in front of her stomach with her right hand.

Matt couldn't keep himself from grinning.

Still in position to play "air guitar," Sarah turned around. Seeing him still at the counter, her cheeks flushed beet red. For a second, her hands froze. Then she abruptly whipped them behind her back. "I'm so embarrassed. I didn't know you were there. I was going to bring everything to you at the table."

The grin didn't leave Matt's face. "It's okay. I sometimes do that when I'm working on something new too."

It was almost as though a lightbulb went on over her head as she realized he played guitar too.

"You know, I can't figure out the next chord in that song."

"If you quit where I think you did, that should be a C-major seventh."

She wiggled her fingers, froze again, then stared at him blankly.

He turned around, moving so she could see the back of his left hand, then lowered his hand to show her his finger position. As she watched, he made the chord in the air. Rather than strum his right hand in front of him, Matt pressed his hand on his stomach and peeked at her over his shoulder. "It goes like this."

"I can't figure that out without the guitar in my hands. I'm not very good. How long have you been playing?"

"Since I was sixteen. So I guess that makes fourteen years, although I don't play as often as I like." He paused, not knowing how his next words would be taken but, at the same time, knowing he should be speaking out for his faith more than he did. "The only times I seem to play anymore is when I'm doing a special number at church, which isn't very often."

Her eyes widened. "I have a friend who goes to that big church across from the arena. Do you go there? Do you know Gwen Bradshaw? And her husband, Lionel? They just had a baby girl a couple of months ago. They named her Jessica."

"Yes, that's where I go. The names sound familiar, but I can't say I know them. It's a big place."

Before he could comment further, Ty returned.

From her response, he had to assume that Sarah didn't attend anywhere and was not a Christian, but she at least she had some friends who were Christians.

Rather than respond to his comment, she finished preparing the two cups of coffee and set them beside the two muffins. She smiled exactly the same as she always did and slid the tray closer to the edge of the counter. "Enjoy!" she chorused, and stepped back. Matt picked everything up, and headed to their usual table.

Ty smiled as he slid in, taking the seat backing up to the wall. "Just one more day, and we're off. This cycle we get the whole weekend. I can hardly wait. Got plans?"

Matt nodded, thinking of his short conversation with Sarah. "I plan to sleep most of Saturday, then go to church on Sunday."

"Say a prayer for me, Buddy, that I catch a big one. I'm going fishing with a couple of friends. We rented a boat this time."

"Some time you'll have to come with me to church."

"Maybe. We'll see." Ty shoveled a large portion of his muffin into his mouth, slurped the foam off the top of his coffee, then grinned over top of the cup. "This is good, and this time, I intend to finish the whole thing before we get called out."

❧

Sarah Cunningham watched the constables take their usual seats, the center table along the wall at the side of the room.

Many RCMP officers came into Donnie's for their breaks. She especially looked forward to seeing Constable Walker. She'd counted out his two days, two nights, four days off schedule, and marked it on her calendar at home, just so she knew in advance when to expect him.

Constable Walker smiled at something the other officer said, then he took a deep and obviously satisfying sip of his coffee.

They'd never done anything but make small talk, some

nights more than others. Today was the first time he'd said anything truly personal.

He played guitar, and he went to church.

Sarah remembered going to church with an elderly neighbor as a child. As an adult, she'd gone once with her friend Gwen. Twice if she counted Gwen and Lionel's wedding.

Knowing a little bit about Constable Walker's life when he was out of uniform put a whole new slant to his character. It certainly made him more interesting as a person, and she already found him quite appealing. Like most officers who came in for their breaks, she supposed the way he held himself and his unshakable confidence and poise went with the uniform. At the same time, something was different about Constable Walker— she just wished she could figure out what it was.

Kristie appeared from the kitchen. "Time for your break, Sarah."

Sarah glanced up at the clock. Even though the two constables had been there for only fifteen minutes, their radios could go off any second, and they'd be gone in an instant. She wanted to talk to Constable Walker, but Donnie didn't allow the staff to sit with the customers while in uniform.

She could go to the back and change, but by the time she did that, they'd likely be gone.

Or. . .she could simply stand. There was no rule about not being friendly with the customers. The guitar-playing RCMP officer with the captivating smile and gorgeous blue eyes was definitely a customer.

She'd been standing all night, and she really needed to sit for a while, but she couldn't wipe the grin off her face as she walked to their table.

They stopped talking when she came to a halt beside them.

"Sorry to interrupt, but can I ask you something, Constable Walker?"

She tried to ignore the sudden ear-to-ear grin of Constable Edwards, who appeared to be fifteen years senior to Constable Walker.

Constable Walker leaned forward, smiled politely, and folded his hands on the table. His sky-blue eyes sparkled, even in the stark fluorescent lighting. "Ask anything you want."

Are you married?

Sarah stood and blinked down at him, not knowing where the thought came from. It had been so clear she couldn't tell for sure she hadn't actually said it out loud.

Fortunately, he continued to look up at her, his expression unchanged. Sarah inhaled sharply. "I was wondering if you could help me with that C-major seventh." She slid a pen and a napkin across the table toward him. "Would you draw it for me?"

As he drew the chord, he explained the fingering, then slid the napkin back toward her. "Do you have an electric guitar or acoustic, Sarah?"

"It's an acoustic guitar with a pickup, although I've never plugged it in. So far, I've only played by myself. And for Gwen, my friend who is teaching me, the one who goes to the same church as you."

"I'm sorry, I don't know who she is, but I'll watch for her next Sunday." He paused for a second, one eyebrow quirked, and he started to open his mouth, making Sarah afraid that he was going to ask if she was going to be at church too. She believed in God as the creator of the universe and all that, but she wasn't about to go to church because of it.

Constable Edwards' radio suddenly blared, cutting off whatever Constable Walker was going to say.

"12Bravo9," a female voice said flatly.

Constable Edwards reached up to press the button "12Bravo9."

"MVA at River Road and Shay Street. Three cars, possible injuries. Can you attend as first responder?"

He turned his head and spoke into the radio, which was fastened just below the tip of his collar. "I'm on my way."

The same female voice came over Constable Walker's radio. "16Bravo4."

He also turned his head as he pushed the button. "16Bravo4."

"Please accompany 12Bravo9."

"16Bravo4 copy. I heard the location."

Both officers stood. They finished their remaining coffees in one gulp and shoveled the last portions of their muffins into their mouths at once.

"Sorry, Sarah," Constable Walker mumbled through his mouthful as he plunked his hat on his head. "Maybe I'll see you tomorrow."

Before she could reply, they were out the door. The two squad cars roared to life. The headlights blinked on, the red and blue lights began to flash, and the sirens blared as they entered the street. Within seconds, they were gone.

Sarah sighed. Once, Constable Walker had told her that they never really knew what they were walking into until they got there. This time, he wouldn't know if this accident was a fender-bender, if it were so serious that people had been badly hurt, or if they were even dead at the scene. As emotionally unsettling as such a thing would be, this time there would be no danger to the attending officers.

For other calls, he could be putting his life on the line.

She didn't want to think of Constable Walker, the officer with the mesmerizing blue eyes, being hurt on the job, or worse. Sarah stared blankly out the window in the last spot she'd seen his car and wondered, even though she didn't go to church, if praying for his safety would be okay.

Sarah sighed and glanced at her wristwatch. She had another five minutes of her break left, but it would be a full twenty-four hours before she might see Constable Walker again.

It was going to be a very long night and an even longer day tomorrow.

two

When Constables Walker and Edwards came to Donnie's Donuts Thursday night, Sarah smiled and waved. Constable Walker tipped his hat and waved back as he walked, not breaking stride as he approached the counter.

"How are you doing with that C-major seventh?"

"I think I've got it figured out. Gwen will be so proud of me. Thank you."

He smiled back. "Any time." He tipped his head to look up at the menu board. "I'm going to take my chances today and order a sandwich. I'm starving, and I forgot my lunch at home. So I'll have a Chicken Supreme and a regular coffee. If I get a call, I can always finish it in the car. It's happened before."

She turned to Constable Edwards and waited as he read the menu board.

"I'll just have a bran muffin and a medium coffee. It figures he'd order a meal when it's my turn to pay."

While she accepted his money and Kristie made the sandwich, Sarah chatted with Constable Walker about the challenges of learning a new instrument. He snickered and told her about the time his B-string snapped in the middle of a song in which he was accompanying a soloist for his church's last Easter Cantata. Sarah laughed, telling him she knew that would never happen to her, not because she knew she would never have a string snap, but because she knew she would never be good enough to play for an audience.

Since Constable Walker was eating and not merely snacking today, she left him alone. Even though she wanted to hear more of his stories, she went into the back of the building to the staff lunchroom instead of disturbing the two men.

As she walked away, she mentally kicked herself for worrying about him the day before. The man was a police officer. He faced dangerous situations all the time. Besides, even though they tended to chat a lot and they saw each other frequently, she really didn't know him.

She could admit she found him attractive. He was a good-looking man, physically fit, and approximately her age. He had a good-paying job, and he was pleasant. Sarah couldn't help but smile, even though she was technically alone. She supposed she found him pleasant because she was on the right side of the law. She doubted the Ronsky clan and their followers found him, or any member of the police force, "friendly."

By the time her fifteen minutes were up, the two officers were gone. On her way to clean up the table they had vacated, she noticed a broken cup under the table where the Ronsky clan had been.

To save herself a trip, Sarah left the table as it was, turned around, and headed for the closet. Unfortunately, the lightbulb had burnt out during the day shift, and no one had replaced it. The broom was easy to find, but with the minimal glow reflecting from the kitchen being her only source of light, she couldn't find the dustpan. She groped along the shelf where it usually was stored until she touched the handle. Unfortunately, because she was smacking her palm down in her attempts to find it, rather than gripping the handle, all she did was knock it to the floor.

The plastic clunked as it landed on the hard vinyl floor, bounced a couple of times, hit her foot, and then slid under the bottom shelf.

Sarah lowered herself to her hands and knees, then down to her elbows, then to the ground until one cheek pressed against the vinyl flooring so she could see beneath the bottom shelf. It was darker on the floor than at standing height, so despite her efforts, she couldn't see anything at all. However, she really needed that dustpan before someone came in, stepped on the broken glass, and sued Donnie for some kind of injury.

She sucked in a deep breath and reached underneath the shelf, hoping that the cleaning staff was as diligent in the storage areas as they were in the restaurant.

Feeling nothing, Sarah gritted her teeth and groped further. After a while, her fingertips brushed the dustpan's handle. Since her arm wasn't quite long enough, Sarah shuffled around, grabbed the broom, and laid it on the floor. She slid it toward the dustpan, intending to knock it forward once she was able to maneuver both herself and the long wooden broom handle in the small closet.

Suddenly, a glowing light in the shape of a rectangle appeared on the wall behind the shelf. She realized it was a vent cover. From her strange position on the floor looking upward through it, she could see into her boss's private office. Donnie had just walked inside and closed the door behind him.

The small amount of light filtering through the grille allowed Sarah to see what she was doing. Ignoring her boss, Sarah aimed the broom toward the vagrant dustpan, which was so far under the shelf that it was against the wall.

Just as she was about to knock it out, she heard Donnie's voice.

Sarah froze. Unlike the rest of the donut shop, Donnie's office was completely silent because Donnie had muted the speaker for the radio station from coming into his office. No one besides Donnie was in the room. He was speaking into the phone. Not the regular phone on his desk, but his cell phone.

"They're gone, and they won't be back tonight," he mumbled quietly. "You can come in now. Have you got it all? Good."

Donnie flipped the phone shut, shuffled sideways while he clipped the unit onto his belt, and waited.

Sarah's mind raced. Only two groups of people had recently left—the Ronsky clan and the two RCMP officers. If the Ronskys were bored or got a case of the munchies after their activities, they had been known to return. There were never any guarantees that they wouldn't be back. As unsavory as they were, they were regular customers, and they always paid cash for their orders.

On the other hand, once Constables Walker and Edwards left, they never came back in the same twenty-four hour period.

Sarah's heart pounded. She didn't know whom Donnie was talking to or why it was important the police officers weren't coming back, but she had a terrible feeling that, whatever the reason, she didn't want to know. All she knew for certain was that she didn't want to know any more than she already did.

Still on her hands and knees, Sarah began to shuffle backward, but her rear end bumped the shelf on the other side of the closet. Something rattled on impact. Because her right hand was still trapped beneath the shelf holding the broom, Sarah winced and covered her head with her left hand, waiting for something to fall.

Her heart pounded. She was less afraid of being hurt than being discovered, because this didn't sound like a conversation Donnie would have wanted any of the staff to overhear.

The objects on the shelf behind her settled. Again, all was deathly silent.

Donnie's door opened, the click of footsteps on the tile floor echoed slightly, and the door closed. The distinct snick of the lock confirmed that the ensuing conversation was indeed meant to be private.

Sarah opened her mouth to breathe as quietly as she could, using short, shallow breaths. She didn't want to look but her eyes refused to stay closed. She didn't know who the man was who had entered, but she recognized him from coming to see Donnie before. Until now, because she worked a regular night shift, she hadn't thought it unusual that Donnie would have visitors so late. After all, these hours were normal for her. However, a sudden sensation of fear enveloped her as she realized that personal visitors at 4:00 A.M. were not standard practice for friends or business.

The man deposited a soft-sided brown leather briefcase onto Donnie's desk. "I'll be back on Tuesday. I expect you to meet your side of the bargain."

Without speaking, Donnie opened the safe in the wall behind his desk, tucked the briefcase inside, and closed the safe's door.

The second Donnie spun the lock, the man turned and left without saying another word. As soon as the door closed, Donnie opened one of the desk drawers and picked up a gun. He checked the clip for ammunition, laid it back in the drawer, and locked it.

Sarah's heart pounded. She didn't know the ramifications of what she had just seen, but something was very wrong. She could probably convince herself that whatever was in the briefcase could simply be valuable versus illegal, but seeing Donnie with a gun chilled her to her core.

The second Donnie left the office, Sarah nudged the dustpan out from beneath the shelf and stood. Quickly, she brushed herself off so no one could tell she'd been on the floor. Very cautiously and very slowly, she peeked out of the closet. When she was sure that no one saw her, she tiptoed out and closed the door quietly behind her.

Instead of going into the food area to sweep up, she ran into the staff room with the broom and dustpan so Donnie wouldn't know where she'd just been.

While she stood in the middle of the vacant staffroom, Donnie's voice echoed from the front counter.

"Kristie, I'm going to be out for about half an hour. Where's Sarah?"

"She's on her break. Want me to get her?"

"No. Just tell her I'm gone, and if anyone phones for me, take a message."

Without further explanation, Donnie left the building.

In a flash, Sarah hid the broom and dustpan behind the door and flopped herself down on the small couch. She was sure her hair hadn't yet settled from the sudden movement when Kristie appeared in the doorway.

"Donnie had to go somewhere. It's my turn for a break. If anyone phones for him, take a message."

Sarah nodded and stood. "Sure. No problem," she said, try-ing her best to keep her voice from shaking. Leaving the broom and dustpan hidden behind the door, she left the staff room and took her place at the front counter. She didn't like to leave the broken mug on the floor, but at not quite 4:30 A.M., the morning crowd hadn't begun to enter yet. For now, she could pick up the large pieces by hand. As soon as Kristie left the staff room, she would retrieve the broom so Kristie wouldn't associate that she'd been anywhere near the closet five minutes ago.

On Tuesday, when the man came back, Sarah also had no intentions of being anywhere near the closet. But still, when the man came back, even if she didn't see what was going on, she knew something was.

Sarah counted on her fingers. Today had been the last shift of Constable Walker's rotation. She wanted to tell him what she'd seen, but he wouldn't be there on Tuesday. With the rotation of his shifts, she wouldn't see him until Thursday night, if he had time to take a break, which he didn't always. For sure, she wouldn't see him Friday night, because she started her "day" at midnight, and therefore, she didn't work Friday nights.

Sarah closed her eyes to picture her calendar. At this point in the rotation cycle, his nightshifts would be on her week-ends, so she wouldn't see him.

She stared blankly at the wall. Donnie's friend's words echoed over and over in her head.

She could only wait.

three

Matt encouraged a group of people to shuffle to the center of the pew. Then he directed an elderly couple to take the now-vacant spaces on the aisle seat. He smiled, expressed his best wishes that they would enjoy the service, and returned to his position at the center entrance to the sanctuary.

He'd arrived earlier than usual today. Normally, he kept an eye on things Sunday mornings when he was ushering, but this time he'd been more diligent in watching the crowd.

Today, he was looking for a young family whose names were Gwen, Lionel, and Jessica. He didn't know what they looked like because he hadn't had time to browse through the church photo directory, but he did know the baby would be approximately two months old. He didn't intend to say anything to them if he did manage to identify them. He was only curious because they were Sarah's friends.

As Matt watched, a young lady entered the building. By the way she looked around the building, it was obvious that she'd never been there before.

He smiled as she approached him. She wore a modest pink dress topped by a light, waist-length jacket. Her shoes were the exact same pink as the dress. In her hair, she wore some kind of matching fluffy fabric adornment.

Overall, she was feminine and pretty. Her light brown hair was shoulder length and framed her face nicely, even if it was a bit unruly. As she came even closer, he was drawn by the color of her eyes—a unique shade of green that was quite uncommon, yet he'd seen those eyes recently. He tried hard to remember where. Since it obviously wasn't at church, the next place he could think of was at the bank, although he usually used the drive-thru bank machine.

He ran through a mental checklist of the cashiers at the supermarket as he continued to study her, trying not to make it obvious that he was watching.

He thought he was doing well until she turned and looked straight at him.

Suddenly, Matt stiffened from head to toe.

The pointy little chin. The delicate cheeks. Judging from the height of her heels, she was five feet, five inches tall.

She stopped and studied him. Her eyes widened even more. He did know those eyes. He saw them once a week, sometimes twice if he was lucky. However, he'd never seen her in "real" clothes and without her hair pulled back. He'd never seen her wear make-up, but today she wore just enough to highlight her best features, especially those unusual eyes.

She gave him a bright, warm smile. "I see I came to the right place."

"Sarah? What are you doing here?" He shook his head and forced himself to smile. "I'm sorry. I didn't mean that the way it sounded. I'm glad you came. Would you like to have a seat?"

She stepped forward a couple of feet into the sanctuary and stopped. Moving only her head, she scanned the large room, which seated nine hundred people on an average Sunday morning.

"That would be nice. Where are you sitting?" Suddenly her face turned beet red, and she covered her cheeks with her palms. "I'm so sorry. If you're already sitting with someone else. . .your family. . ." Her voice trailed off.

Matt thought of his mother and father, who were attending their own church back in Toronto, where he had been born and raised. "No, my family lives in. . ." He let his own voice trail off as it dawned on him what she meant. He felt his own cheeks heat up, probably matching hers. "I'm here alone. I'm not married. We can sit together if you'd like."

"Are you sure? I can go sit with Gwen and Lionel." She turned her head and scanned the growing crowd already seated in the sanctuary. "They don't know I'm coming, but they've got to be here somewhere. I really wanted to talk to you, though. Can I ask you something after the service? There's something I'm not sure of, and I didn't know how to get in touch with you through the police station." She fidgeted with her purse, studying it intently as she did so. "I don't mean to intrude on your time off." She turned her head to look at the door. Matt wondered if she were about to bolt.

Matt held his hands out. "It's okay, Sarah. How about if we go out for lunch after the service, and you can tell me then what's on your mind."

She smiled so sweetly that her relief was almost tangible. "Thank you, Constable Walker. That's perfect."

He grinned. "Please, my name is Matt. I'm not on duty now." He ran his hand down his tie, then smoothed the lapel of his suit.

Behind him, he could hear the door open and close. Sarah looked behind him. "You may not be on duty, but you are ushering. I should leave you alone. More people just walked in."

Matt turned. He smiled and nodded at the newcomers. "Hi Brad, Selina."

"Hi, Matt." Brad and Selina glanced briefly at Sarah, smiled and nodded at her, and walked past them into the sanctuary.

"Not everyone needs to be escorted in. But this is your first time here, so you do. Since I'm ushering, I'll be standing near the door until about ten minutes after the start of the service. If you like, you can sit here, at the end of the last pew. I can join you after everything gets started."

Their eyes met. She smiled at him, her face the picture of sweetness.

Matt's throat went dry. The same friendly face from the donut shop was smiling at him, but everything else had changed. She looked so different out of the unisex, shapeless blue smock of the donut shop. At Donnie's Donuts, she looked like just another clerk, not unlike anyone else working in any donut shop in town. Today, in the setting of his church, she was an attractive woman, a real person among his friends and Christian brothers and sisters.

"I'll just sit down now, and I'll see you again when you're done."

Without waiting for him to move, Sarah picked a bulletin out of the pile in his hand, sidestepped around him, and sat in the closest empty aisle seat. Once seated, she looked back at him over her shoulder, waved, and faced the front.

Matt stared at the back of her head. He doubted it was a coincidence that her presence at church immediately followed his admission that he attended regularly. At the time, she'd commented that she knew people who went to the same church as he did, but she didn't say that she attended regularly elsewhere. The omission made him nervous. She'd already admitted that she wanted to talk to him about something, confirming that she wasn't there to seek God. She was there to seek him.

He'd been down that road before with a woman, and he wouldn't do it again.

Regardless, he had promised to take her out for lunch, and since he wasn't completely sure about her faith, he decided to give her the benefit of the doubt.

For the remainder of the time until the service started, he greeted people at the door and escorted many to their seats as required. When the lights dimmed and the stream of people dwindled, he quietly walked into the foyer and to one of the other entrances to the sanctuary.

"Dave, I need a favor."

Dave smiled. "Sure. What's up?"

"Someone I wasn't expecting came today, and I want to sit with her. Can you check the halls for me and keep an eye on things?"

"No problem. Enjoy the service."

Matt smiled, but he wasn't sure he would. He knew he would be distracted. Whenever it was his turn to usher, he kept an eye on the hallways during the service. Sometimes opportunistic thieves wandered into the church midway through the service hoping to find an unlocked and unoccupied room full of things to steal while everyone's attention was elsewhere.

Matt stood at the rear of his designated aisle until the ushers were called forward to take up the offering. When everything was done, he made his way to the sound room with the other ushers, where they put all the bags into the safe. After he made sure the door was locked properly, he walked back into the sanctuary. Instead of taking up his usual position, he sat beside Sarah.

She shifted to make room for him and smiled as he tucked his Bible under his seat. He then joined in with the congregation as everyone sang a couple more worship songs.

Most of the time he could make the adjustment from the security in the hallway to focusing his thoughts and heart on the Lord, but not today.

Today, he could concentrate only on Sarah. While he often saw people who didn't sing much or at all, it was rather obvious that Sarah didn't know any of the songs. Even though Matt suspected her only reason for being there was because of him, Matt said a quick prayer for her. If Sarah wasn't at that moment a believer, he prayed that she would be moved by the words, which were about God's love and forgiveness.

The sermon centered on the same topic, which Matt thought perfect for a non-believer to hear. He didn't know if she owned a Bible, but since she hadn't brought one, he shared his, pointing to the text when the pastor began to read.

Her eyebrows rose as he paged to the next passage. She leaned closer to him and whispered. "You've written stuff in your Bible. In pen. Is that allowed?"

Matt smiled. "If I make notes on the backs of the weekly bulletins, it's too much like filing my reports. I'll remember some, but I could never remember everything, especially once it's filed. If Pastor Colin says something that really hits me, I write it in my Bible so I'll see it again the next time I'm reading on that

All he could do was stare at her. "Defensive. . . Sarah, I wish there was something I could do or say, but you really haven't got anything I can follow up on. I can't arrest someone for looking creepy. You have no proof, or even reasonable grounds that something illegal is going on. We can't spend the manpower to investigate why a business owner would put a briefcase into a safe, or why he would have a gun in a locked drawer if he's the registered owner. But if you really can say for sure something definable is happening, then the proper thing to do is to go down to the station and file a complaint or fill out a suspicious persons report if you can identify the perpetrator."

"I can't do that. That's why I came to you. I wanted to know what to do."

"Unfortunately, you can't report a crime until it happens. There's nothing you can do except keep an eye on things. When something happens, then please report it, by all means. Or do the same as you just did. Talk to me when you see something unusual. I'll do my best to help. If you need something checked out, I can do that. First, I can check and see if Donnie has a gun registered to his name. Even if he doesn't, before I can do anything, I'd need to get a search warrant. I'd need a good reason to do that, and then he'd find out you were watching him. You don't want that. For all you know, if you didn't see it that well, it may not have been a gun at all. He could have been changing the battery in his cell phone. You'd be surprised what people *think* they see in situations like what you just experienced. Would you be able to identify that specific gun if we lined up three or four pistols in a row?"

Her eyebrows rose. "I doubt it. I didn't see it that well."

"Until we can ascertain what's happening, all you can do is keep quiet and be careful. It could be nothing. For all we know, it could be a family heirloom in that briefcase, and the only bargain is Donnie agreed to keep it locked up."

"I had a bad feeling you were going to say that. I'm glad I

asked you before I went into the police station and made a fool of myself."

Strangely, at that moment he felt proud of her, that she was thinking of making a report, even though she had nothing concrete to stand on. If more citizens reported suspicious activity when there was something worthwhile to follow up, then the police would have a better chance at catching the bad guys. Too many people turned a blind eye when they saw something wrong. Yet, those were the same people who blamed the police for doing nothing and being caught unaware when something major happened and no one saw it coming.

In this instance, in his gut, he suspected Sarah was probably right. In his experience, when an employee had a bad feeling something funny was going on behind the scenes, there usually was. However, since Sarah hadn't witnessed anything concrete, and since they had no evidence of a criminal act, she was best to stay in the background—watching.

Since she still appeared nervous, Matt thought it a good time to change the subject to something less threatening. What he really wanted was to gauge her reaction to the service and to see where she sat spiritually, but this wasn't the right timing because her mind was obviously on other things.

For the rest of their afternoon together, he changed the subject to distract her from being frightened. He gave her some tips on playing guitar and recommended a few beginner books when he found out she only owned one so far.

Once they were finished eating and ready to leave, Matt escorted her to her car. He stepped close, wishing he could do something to prove her fears were not unfounded and find something on which the force could begin a genuine investigation. Yet he was bound by rules and regulations. For now, all he could do was give her advice, and he wasn't comfortable with that. She was different from the average civilian. She was. . .Sarah.

"Remember, if you see or hear anything, no matter how

small, and even if it seems insignificant, talk to me about it. I'll be able to tell you when it's time to file a report. Just be careful and don't do anything foolish." He grinned and splayed one hand over the center of his chest. "That's my job."

She smiled and reached to him, resting her hand on his arm. "Thank you, Matt. It feels so funny after all this time to call you by your first name. I'll do that. I want to thank you for taking the time to talk to me. Especially, thank you for buying my lunch. I owe you one."

He smiled back. "No problem. I'll see you in a few nights. Until then, stay safe."

four

By the time Thursday came, Sarah was a nervous wreck. All night long, every time the door opened, she nearly dropped what she was holding.

Donnie's creepy acquaintance had reappeared on Tuesday night, just as he said he would. This time Kristie let him into Donnie's office, and then he was gone so quickly Sarah hadn't had time to listen from the closet. She hadn't been able to get a better description of him for Matt, but she did see that this time he hadn't carried anything into Donnie's office, nor did he take the briefcase back.

That didn't mean everything was well. In fact, Sarah suspected the opposite was true. For the hour following the man's visit, Donnie had acted funny. He'd even yelled at poor Kristie for something that wasn't her fault. Today, Sarah had answered a call for Donnie that she thought was the same voice as the visitor. Donnie hadn't come out of his office for an hour afterwards, which again told her something wasn't right.

Sarah had almost worked herself into a tizzy when, at 4:00 A.M., her wishes were answered.

She put on her best smile, even though she was shaking inside. "Hi, Ma. . .uh. . .Constable Walker. And Constable. . ." She leaned closer to the other officer's nametag. "Lawrence. What can I get for you gentlemen today?"

Matt smiled brightly. "I'll have a blueberry muffin and a medium coffee."

The other officer nodded. "Same for me."

Sarah left the two men at the counter while she fetched the muffins and poured the coffee. The urge to tell Matt about Donnie's strange actions was so strong it was almost painful.

However, not only was Matt with someone, Donnie could have been around the corner listening.

She made polite chitchat with Matt while he paid, and both officers walked to a table.

This time, they stayed only inside for ten minutes and left without their radios going off, which Sarah thought odd. Something fluttered inside her stomach when she thought Matt smiled at her from across the restaurant as he walked toward the exit. She wished he could have stayed longer, which didn't make sense. All she could do was look at him from across the room unless he called her to either clean something up or ask her a question.

As soon as they left, Sarah began to clear their table. While she worked, she glanced up and through the large windows, then did a double take. The two squad cars were still in the lot. Constable Lawrence was half sitting on the hood of his squad car, smoking a cigarette. Matt was standing upwind while the two of them talked.

Rather than gawk, she bent to clean the table. Her hand froze as she reached for the empty cups. A pen with the RCMP logo on it was on the seat where Matt had been.

She straightened and looked out the window. Constable Lawrence discarded his cigarette and was opening his squad car's door. Matt, on the other hand, was standing in one place, his hat in his hands while he picked at something on the brim.

Sarah turned to Kristie, who was now standing behind the till. "One of the officers forgot something. If I run, I can catch them."

Without waiting for Kristie to reply, Sarah grabbed the pen and dashed outside. Matt had just opened his car door, but he wasn't yet inside. "Wait! You forgot something!"

He smiled. "I was wondering when you were going to find that. Now that we're out of earshot of any flies on the wall, did anything happen this week?"

"Yes and no. That man came in on Tuesday, and he also

phoned today. I didn't see or hear anything, but Donnie acted really funny both times. I know something is up."

"I believe you. I just need something more than that to start investigating. I don't want him to get suspicious if you're out here talking to me too long, so you'd better get back inside. Keep me posted, okay?" He paused and glanced toward the building. "And Sarah, remember, stay safe."

"You bet."

Sarah handed him the pen and ran inside while Matt drove off.

The officers hadn't been gone more than ten minutes, when Donnie's illusive "friend" entered with another briefcase. Donnie was already waiting for him near the opening to his office door. Without a word spoken between the two of them, they disappeared inside, and the door closed.

Sarah's breath caught in her throat. She turned around to see if anyone were watching her. The only person nearby was Kristie. Since the muffins for the next day were already in the oven, Kristie was stacking donuts in the trays behind her.

"Kristie, can you watch things for a minute? I have to go do something."

Kristie nodded without turning around. "Sure."

Sarah hurried to the closet, slipped inside, and closed the door without turning the light on. She dropped to her hands and knees and angled her head so she could see upwards through the metal grille of the vent.

The man had put the briefcase down on Donnie's desk, but his hand still remained on the handle. "What do you mean, you're not ready for more? We agreed on a date."

Donnie's voice came out much softer and lower in pitch than usual. Sarah shuffled closer to the vent, straining to hear.

"You gave me more than we agreed on. I need more time."

"I'll mention that to Lennie, and I'll let you know what he says on Monday."

The man started to turn around, then shuffled back. "Unless you promise you can give me back my case Monday, empty.

Then I can make an excuse for you."

Donnie nodded frantically. "I'd appreciate that."

The man turned back to face Donnie. "Consider it a favor. You only get one."

Donnie stiffened all over. His voice came out in a croak. "Thanks, Blair. I understand."

Since the conversation was over or at least as much as she needed to hear, Sarah jumped to her feet, grabbed the broom without the dustpan, and ran into the kitchen. She knew she'd never make it into the restaurant area without looking like she was running, so she quickly started sweeping the kitchen, even though everything was already clean.

Kristie appeared in the doorway with an empty tray. When she saw Sarah, she let out a little squeal and nearly dropped the tray. "You scared me! I thought you were going to be in the restaurant."

"I saw something here. But I guess I should probably do around the tables too." Without clarifying, and without the dustpan, Sarah hustled into the main area before Kristie had time to think.

Sarah swept every inch of the floor, but her thoughts were elsewhere. No matter how suspicious things looked, there had been no talk about what the items were that Donnie had received. There had been no talk of money, no deals made, and no talk of another delivery.

Sarah was by no means a detective, but she'd read enough super-spy books to know that she hadn't heard enough for the police to make a report.

But something bad was happening, and something had to be done.

She needed Matt. She walked to the calendar on the wall and counted out his schedule, confirming what she already knew. His upcoming nightshifts were on the weekends. She wouldn't see him for weeks.

With all the dirt and litter in a neat pile, Sarah quietly

retrieved the dustpan from the closet.

Matt wouldn't be coming to her, so she had to go to him.

ஒ

Once again, Sarah sucked in a deep breath for courage, and walked into the lobby of the huge building.

Instead of Matt, another man dressed in a nice suit and tie approached her.

"Welcome!" he said as he held out one hand. "Is this your first time here?"

Sarah shook her head and then slipped her hand into his. "No, actually I was here last week. I'm looking for Matt Walker."

The man raised his eyebrows, then smiled. "Let's go see if we can find him. I know he's here."

Without waiting for her to accept or decline his invitation, he started walking. "Last I saw Matt, he was over there." As they rounded the corner of the hallway, they found Matt in a circle of people, laughing and talking. Unlike the week before, today he wasn't wearing a suit jacket, but he was wearing a nice tie.

"Matt! Someone's here to see you!"

Matt was still half laughing as he turned around. As he saw her, his expression fell. He turned back to the people in the circle. "Excuse me. I'll catch you later."

As he started moving, his friends looked at her. Sarah tried to ignore the butterflies in her stomach at their knowing smiles. As much as she liked Matt, what they thought they "knew" was wrong.

He was at her side within seconds. His voice lowered to almost a whisper, and he rested one hand on her arm.

Sarah looked down. Matt's hand was huge. His fingers nearly wrapped around her arm, and his hand was warm on her skin. His fingers were slightly rough, but his touch was still gentle. For a man, he had lovely hands.

"What's wrong? Did something happen?"

She looked up into his eyes. Beautiful blue eyes, so full of concern that her throat clogged.

Sarah cleared her throat. "He came in again. He brought another briefcase, and he said—"

Matt raised his free hand. "Wait. I'm sorry. I shouldn't have asked that here. This is God's house. It's a place of worship, which is what I came here to do. Let's go out for lunch again. We can talk there. Okay?"

Sarah felt her cheeks heat. "I'm so sorry, Matt. Maybe I should leave."

He smiled again and gave her arm a gentle squeeze. Attractive little crinkles formed at the corners of his gorgeous eyes. "I didn't mean for you to leave. In fact, I'm really glad you came. Everyone is welcome to attend the service, and that means you too. Would you like to sit with me? As usual, I came alone."

"But those people you were talking to?"

"We'll probably all sit together. Let me introduce you."

Everyone smiled nicely as Matt introduced her as his friend, not the clerk at the donut shop, which Sarah liked, even though they were more acquaintances than friends.

"I think it's time to go sit down. This way."

Sarah discreetly checked her watch, which said there were still ten minutes to go until the service started. She quietly followed Matt and his friends into the sanctuary.

They sat in the back row in the center of the large room, which Sarah thought odd. Matt, however, told her that just like sitting in the back row of the movie theater, it was the best spot in the house because from here, he could see everything.

Sarah doubted there would be as much action at the front of the church as on the big screen. At least there hadn't been last week. Her most prominent thought about sitting in the back row of a movie theater was teenagers necking in the dark. She doubted that was what Matt had in mind in church.

Matt bent to tuck his Bible under the pew. Very different out of uniform, he was still in many ways the same. He was gentle, yet firm. Strong, yet kind. He generated authority, yet he wasn't pushy or outspoken. He was also quite a handsome man in normal clothes, although Sarah had to admit that Matt sure looked good in his uniform.

He straightened. Leaning toward her, he spoke softly close to her ear. "We can see pretty much the whole place from here. Do you see your friends?"

Sarah shook her head. "They aren't going to be here this week. Believe it or not, they've left their daughter with Gwen's mother, and they've taken a trip to someplace in the southeastern states. They're attending the anniversary celebration of a little church they discovered when they were new at driving."

She turned to Matt. One eyebrow quirked, but he didn't say a word.

She grinned. "Before their daughter was born, they were both long-haul truck drivers. When Jessica was born, they sold the truck. Lionel took a job in the office so he could stay in town with his new family. I think Gwen is going to stay home for a couple of years, and then she's going to do part-time subbing for a while. She's my friend, the teacher. But she's a truck driver too. And now she's a mother."

"It sounds like you know some very interesting people. You'll have to introduce them to me one day."

Sarah opened her mouth, but no words came out. She wondered if Matt realized his statement implied that she would be back at his church again, after today, perhaps more than once. "I guess," she muttered.

The lights dimmed, a screen lowered from a recessed spot in the ceiling, and the music became louder. A man at the front podium welcomed everyone present, and the congregation stood to sing the first song.

As the first part of the service progressed, Sarah was less nervous than the week before, because she knew what to expect. When the pastor began his message, Matt opened his Bible and pointed to the spot the man was reading. This time, Sarah knew better than to comment on Matt's writing all over the place. She still managed to hear what the pastor was saying, but while he was talking, Sarah couldn't help but admire Matt's neat handwriting. Even though it was supposed to be scribbled notes, his handwriting was quite neat and certainly very readable.

Still, she didn't want to be rude. Sarah stopped looking at Matt's handwriting and raised her head to watch the pastor. As the week before, he was equally as interesting to listen to. She followed his topic enthusiastically, learning a little historical background on how people lived back in the olden Bible days. She found it fascinating that lots of people in the Bible messed up, but God loved them anyway.

When the service was over, they shuffled out with the crowd, then arranged to meet at a designated restaurant.

This time, they had to put their names on a waiting list. Sarah didn't mind. Matt would talk about what she'd seen at Donnie's only in the privacy of their table, where there was no chance of being overheard if they kept their voices down. The wait gave her more of a chance to talk to Matt before he became a cop again.

five

Matt glanced at the crowd around them, anxious to know what Sarah had considered so important that she again would come to church to seek him out.

Regardless of her reason, he was glad she had come to church. He'd enjoyed sitting with her during the service.

He held back a sigh. It was obvious what his friends were thinking when she joined them—he'd seen their little smirks, and he was sure Sarah had too.

As much as he might have liked them to be right, they were wrong. Even though he liked Sarah, he had to keep a professional distance, which was difficult when she came to see him during off-duty hours. If she really had seen something worth investigating, then getting personally involved with a potential witness could jeopardize the case.

Yet, at the same time, he knew he was doing the right thing by encouraging her to come to church. True, she'd come because of him, for reasons that had nothing to do with seeking God, but he'd watched her during the service. She hadn't known a single song, but she'd read the words and not ignored them. Matt figured that was a good start.

At times, she had become distracted during the pastor's sermon. However, her eyes and ears had perked up when Pastor Colin became more focused and centered on his topic of the week, which was about great men of God who made tremendous mistakes. Moses. David. Peter. Pastor had compared them to modern times to show that even though the times had changed, people certainly hadn't. Then and now, people made bad choices. God still loved every one of them.

The whole time, Matt had watched her out of the corner of

his eye. She'd been frozen in her chair. He didn't know why the topic intrigued her, but it did.

Sarah nudged his arm. "I think we're next. Those people were just ahead of us."

Matt rubbed his stomach and grinned. "That's great. I'm starving."

They were soon seated, menus in hand, with a couple of cups of good, hot, fresh coffee in front of them.

Sarah closed her menu and laid it on the table first. "Before I forget, I wanted to tell you I couldn't help but notice your handwriting this morning. Even in what was probably scribbles in the margins and miscellaneous notes written in a rush, everything was so neat and tidy. I guess you write a lot, reports and stuff, don't you?"

Matt closed his menu and laid it down on top of Sarah's. "Not as much as the generation before me. Most of my reports are done on computer, although many are still handwritten." He grinned and folded his hands on the table in front of him. "I can probably type better than you can."

She grinned. "I just might surprise you. How many reports do you do in a day? I find this so interesting."

He shrugged his shoulders. "It varies with what day of the week, and day shift or night shift. I'd say I average twelve to fifteen reports a night."

She leaned closer. "I finally have something you can start a report on. I have a name!"

Just as Matt leaned forward, the waitress appeared. The second she had finished taking their orders and left, Sarah leaned toward Matt. "The guy who came in to see Donnie is named Blair."

"Blair?" Matt's stomach tightened, and the sensation of hunger disappeared. "Blair Kincaid?" The two things he thought most likely to be going on to involve a non-franchised open-all-night restaurant dealt with either drug distribution or money laundering. Both could very likely involve Blair Kincaid. Word at the station was that he was again out on the streets and on their list of people to watch for.

"Donnie didn't say his last name."

Matt picked up his coffee cup, trying to appear mellow. "Did you see him any better this time?"

"No. He came in on Monday or Tuesday, but I couldn't let him see that I was looking at him. I didn't want him to get suspicious."

"That's probably a good idea. If this man is who I think he might be, this is very bad news. Can't you tell me anything about him, even if it's something that seems insignificant to you? Other than the fact that he's got brown hair. Any scars or odd features? Tattoos? Did he have a big nose? Eye color isn't that important. Most witnesses don't see the perp close enough to notice, but those other things can be very helpful in a description."

Sarah shook her head. "The first time he came in this week, all I saw was his back. The other time, I was in the closet again. It's hard to see from down on the floor, up through the vent, and across Donnie's office. But I would recognize his voice if I heard him."

"You've spoken to him but can't describe him?" Matt sucked in a deep breath, then forced himself to breathe evenly. As a police officer, he commonly came across witnesses who couldn't describe a person after not only seeing them, but also talking to them. He didn't want to think that Sarah could be so oblivious to detail, especially when she was supposed to be paying attention.

"But all I did was talk to him. I didn't see him. I spoke with him on the phone. Donnie must not have had his cell on, because once he called on the main line and asked for Donnie. It was the same voice I heard from the closet. Only it was clearer on the phone."

"Well, it's a start. Keep your eyes and ears open. If you can get a last name, or a description, or see what's in those cases that are coming in, then we can take this further and start a report. Just remember to watch from a distance. If this Blair is who I think he is, he's nothing but trouble waiting for a place to happen." Matt prayed quickly that trouble wasn't already happening, but he had a feeling his prayer came too late.

Sarah nodded just as the waitress delivered their meals. Because Matt knew Sarah would not be accustomed to thanking God before she ate, he closed his eyes briefly for a short, silent prayer by himself. Once he tasted his first bite, his appetite renewed.

Sarah bit into her burger then started talking through the food in her mouth. "I feel so much better having talked to you. At least I know I'm not going crazy. Or that I'm not imagining the bad vibes."

"I don't believe in bad vibes, but I do believe in being attuned to what's going on around you, and being able to tell if it's something bad."

"I don't know what it's like at Donnie's during the daytime, or if that Blair guy comes in during the day. I only work at night. Do you think I should ask any of the day people if they've seen him?"

Matt dabbed at his mouth with his napkin to hide his smile. He would like to see her asking people to watch out for someone she couldn't describe. "I don't think that's necessary at this point. Why do you only work nights?"

"I work nights to support myself while I take classes half-time during the day. I'm studying to be a teacher. I'm over halfway through my courses. Remember before, when I mentioned my friend Gwen? She's a teacher, and she loves it. That's why I decided to be a teacher too. Of course it would go faster if I could go to classes full-time, but I can't afford that."

"Still, going to university along with working full-time must completely fill up your days. When do you sleep?"

"It's not as bad a schedule as everyone thinks. My shift at Donnie's is from midnight to 8:00 A.M. I'm there for the dead zone of the middle of the night, and I end after the morning rush, which starts at 5:30 as the commuters start to make their way into Vancouver. I have barely enough time to be at the university by 8:30. I'm finished with classes at noon, and I go straight home to study and do my homework and anything else I have to do. I generally sleep from about two or three in the afternoon until ten or eleven at night, when I get up and start all over again. I tend to catch up on my sleep on the weekends."

"I know from personal experience how tough that must be."

Sarah shrugged her shoulders. "I guess I don't have much of a life, but if this is the way I have to do it to get my university education, then that's the way it's got to be. The pay isn't the best, but it covers my bills while I'm going to school, and the hours suit me." She grinned. "Besides, I get sandwiches at Donnie's for half price when I'm working. Then I don't have to make myself a lunch every day. At least not Monday to Friday. Working nights isn't all bad, once you get used to it and adjust your lifestyle accordingly."

Matt nodded. Police officers everywhere worked the same type of swing shift. Typically, it was two twelve-hour days, two twelve-hour nights, four days off, and the rotation started all over again. The hours came with the job, and there was nothing he could do about it. He knew how difficult it was to try and sleep properly when he was the only one in his apartment building sleeping during the daytime. He didn't want to imagine what it would be like working nights permanently.

They continued to chat about anything not related to Donnie's Donuts until Sarah noticed the restaurant had all but emptied of people.

She leaned forward in the chair and lowered her voice, as if what she was saying was a big secret. "Did you notice the time? There's hardly anyone here anymore. Do you know how long we've been here?"

Matt chuckled. "They know me. Like at Donnie's, they give me free coffee refills and encourage me to stay, in or out of uniform. Come on, let's go."

As they walked together to the car, Matt had to kick himself for feeling chauvinistic. He didn't want to go their separate ways from the public parking lot. He would much rather have driven her home in his car and said goodbye at her front door.

Today he couldn't, but one day, perhaps.

He pulled his wallet and a pen out of his back pocket. "Here's my card. It's got the station's number on it, but I'll give you my home phone number so you can call me any time you want." He paused while he wrote the number down. "My number is unlisted, so I'd appreciate it if you didn't give it out, not even to anyone at Donnie's if anyone else sees something."

"No, I'd never give out someone's number unless they first said it was okay," she said as she accepted the card from him.

Matt opened his mouth, nearly asking for her number in exchange, now that he'd given her his, but he stopped himself. For the kind of relationship that just flitted through his mind, Sarah was off-limits.

He'd turned thirty a few months ago, and he'd already been thinking of marriage for a few years. Knowing that at his age, marriage was a possibility in a relationship, he wasn't going to start out wrong by dating a non-Christian. The woman would have to be a true believer, already having made her commitment to the Lord, before he could entertain the thought. After that, Matt could happily settle for second place.

Matt loved to minister to unbelievers and new believers, but his disastrous relationship with Nanci, his ex-girlfriend, had taught him that dating was not the time to attempt to bring someone into God's Kingdom. Only after their relationship had become serious had Nanci claimed to have become a believer. He found out the hard way that wasn't so. She had lied and said she was a Christian just so he would keep going out with her. Their breakup had been long and painful because he'd let his heart overrule his head.

After that, even though finding a woman who could live with his job as a police officer would be difficult, Matt told himself he would never date a non-Christian woman again. He needed to know that a woman had come to a decision to follow Jesus—independent of any relationship he had with her—and for her own reasons.

If God wanted him to remain single, he would do so. Between his schedule and his job, he didn't date much. If God wanted him to be married, then the right woman, a Christian woman, would be dropped in his path.

Sarah hadn't exactly been dropped in his path, nor was she a Christian. She said she believed in God, but the book of James stated even the demons believed that. The point was they didn't love Jesus and follow His words and teachings with all their hearts.

Therefore, with the rules in place and knowing what had happened before, this time he would not set himself up for a potential heartbreak. He would not even entertain the possibility of a relationship with Sarah, no matter how much he liked her.

Equally important, Sarah was a potential witness. Getting personally involved with her would jeopardize her credibility. As well, emotional involvement could interfere with his ability to take action if needed. He couldn't cross that line. If Donnie's visitor really was the infamous Blair Kincaid, he had reasons of his own for wanting Kincaid off the streets.

Even though he hadn't turned his notes in to the Shift NCO, he had documented what Sarah told him the previous week. Likewise, he would document what she had told him today. Even though it wasn't official yet, this was his baby. He had every intention of seeing it through to the end, which he couldn't do if he were personally involved with the prime witness for the prosecution.

Sarah tilted her head as she looked at him. "Matt? Why are you looking at me like that?"

Immediately, Matt felt a burn in his cheeks. "Sorry. My mind wandered to something else. I guess I'll see you next time I'm breathing black air."

Her brows knotted in the center of her forehead. "Pardon me?"

One corner of Matt's mouth quirked up. "Sorry. That's cop talk for working the night shift."

She smiled and something strange happened in Matt's stomach. "I get it! That's really funny!"

"I wouldn't have called it funny," he mumbled. "I guess I'll see you soon, then. Remember, call me any time you have a question, or if you see anything. Until I see you again, stay safe."

"Will do." She waved the card in the air, then plopped herself behind the wheel of her car, started the engine, and shut the door.

Matt stood in one spot, without moving, watching her drive away. Not that he intended to call her, but he couldn't help but memorize her license plate number. It was now a simple matter to run it through the computer if he needed to. Once he got her driver's license number, he would have access to much of her personal information if he wanted it.

He didn't need her birthday, but he thought he might just need her phone number for his personal report.

six

Sarah selected a variety of donuts for a lady at the drive-thru window, then hurried back to the counter for the restaurant area. "Can I help you, Sir?"

"Hi, Sarah. I'll take one of those chocolate donuts and a medium coffee. When's your next break?" A familiar face grinned at her, but she had to blink hard to let the rest of the package sink in.

Instead of Matt's usually bare head, tonight a baseball cap, which sported the logo of one of the local garages, sat neatly atop his head. Instead of his pristine uniform, he wore a baggy sweatshirt that had seen better days, along with a pair of jeans so faded they were almost white.

Sarah glanced at the clock on the wall, then lowered her voice to barely above a whisper. "Matt? What are you doing here?"

His grin widened. "What? I'm not allowed to buy donuts on my day off? And you'll notice I really am buying a donut today, instead of the usual muffin."

Sarah smiled back at him. "It's four in the morning. I'm surprised, but glad you're here. Let me see what Kristie is doing. I can probably take a break now. I'll be right with you."

She quickly filled his order, then hustled to the kitchen where Kristie was standing at the opening to the donut cooker, watching the current batch of donuts make their way through the process. "Would you mind keeping an eye on the front counter? A friend is here, and I'm going to take a coffee break."

"No problem."

Sarah ran into the staff room and shut the door while she released her hair from the ponytail and changed from her Donnie's Donuts smock to the blouse she'd been wearing when she arrived. She was still stuffing her blouse into the waistband of her pants as she reached for the doorknob. In record time, she made it into the restaurant to join Matt. Instead of his usual table, she found him sitting where he could watch both the main door and the path to Donnie's office without being obvious about it.

He grinned. "How do you like my disguise?"

She grinned back. "It's not much of a disguise. Where are the sunglasses? I thought cops wore sunglasses when they didn't want to be recognized."

"It's the middle of the night. Wearing sunglasses would draw attention, and I don't want anyone looking at me. Besides, I'm indoors. I'm dressed like this so Donnie won't recognize me. I've never been here in civilian clothes. I don't know why, but most people don't recognize me the first time they see me out of uniform."

"You know, you're right." Sarah remembered the first time she'd seen him out of uniform—at his church, the first time she'd gone. Even though she was deliberately looking for him, she had barely recognized him. His mono-colored tailored suit was probably the closest normal clothes could be to a uniform, and she'd had to look twice. The ratty sweatshirt and worn jeans were quite ordinary for the late night crowd, but not for Matt, who had never been there at night in anything but his pristine uniform.

"Good thinking." Sarah shifted in her seat so her back was deliberately toward the door of Donnie's office. Even though she was also currently not wearing her uniform, she didn't want Donnie to notice her either. "I haven't seen much of Donnie today. I guess he's been busy."

Matt nodded. "I can see that. He usually leaves the door ajar about six inches when he's in his office, but today it's fully closed."

Sarah turned around and glanced quickly at the closed door, then turned back to Matt. "How do you know he's in there?"

"I can see a crack of light under the door. When he's not in the office, he turns the light out."

"Oh. I never thought of that."

"It's my job to notice those things. Sometimes it's how I stay alive."

Her happy mood vanished as fast if someone had thrown a pail of cold water over her head. Of course, she knew cops had dangerous jobs. They did more than hand out speeding tickets and tell rowdy teenagers to keep the volume down on Saturday nights. Glamorous Hollywood-style television shows and James Bond movies aside, cops really did face unpredictable and dangerous situations often.

Except for going to his church, Sarah had never seen Matt outside the calm, protected atmosphere of Donnie's Donuts. Since she'd come to know and like him, she blocked the possibilities of Matt facing danger out of her mind. Police officers did get injured and even killed in the line of duty. Reality was often ugly. Matt probably saw things on a regular basis she'd never imagined in her worst nightmares.

"Why did you become a cop?"

His eyebrows rose, and he leaned back in the chair. "I don't really know. I've always wanted to be in the RCMP from as far back as I can remember. It might have had something to do with our neighbor when I was a kid. He was RCMP, and he was such a nice guy, always helping people, even on his days off. My parents adored him as much as us kids. He was just an all-around around great guy, and we all really looked up to him. Of course, we were all even more impressed whenever we saw him in his uniform. Back then, they were more formal than they are today. I remember one day he spoke at our school. All the kids were in awe of him. Of course, I was ever so proud, at seven years old, to say I knew him. Between my neighbor and my parents, with my upbringing, they really instilled a sense of right and wrong in me. Following my neighbor's footsteps into the RCMP seemed like the natural thing to do."

Sarah plunked her elbows on the table and rested her chin in her palms. "That's so interesting."

"I don't know about that. Everyone makes his or her career choice for different reasons. Why do you want to become a teacher? I'm sure it's not just because you have a friend who is a teacher."

"No. I love kids, and it's something I've wanted to do since high school. I used to help out at the local elementary school a few hours a week as part of one of my courses. When I graduated I couldn't afford the university; I had to get a job right away to support myself. It was Gwen who told me how I could do it part-time and gave me the push I needed to actually work toward my degree. She's been helping me a lot with assignments and stuff. I have a feeling she also talked to the administrator at the university for me."

"It sounds like you've known her for a long time."

Sarah smiled. "Yes, we went to high school together. Do you still see anyone you went to school with?"

Matt shook his head. "Most cops aren't stationed where they grew up. When we finish training, we're shipped out wherever there is an opening. Most of the time, we stay there unless we put in for a transfer. I didn't grow up or go to school here. I grew up in Toronto. After I finished my training, this is where they sent me. I'm okay, but a lot of the guys feel really displaced. It's hard to get to know people when you do shift work, and you tend to lose track of people easily when you move away and life gets busy. Praise God for E-mail."

Sarah suddenly felt sad for him. She reached out and rested her fingers on his arm. He stiffened for a second beneath her touch but otherwise didn't move. Nothing on his face changed to indicate surprise, discomfort, or even pleasure at her touch. "It must be so hard, being here all alone. To make it worse, I know doing shift work doesn't help your social life. Working graveyard hours hasn't exactly done wonders for mine."

He smiled, and with his free hand, he reached over and patted her hand that was on top of his left arm. His hand stilled and stayed where it was, pinning her hand beneath it. The warmth of his touch did strange things to her insides. "I'm doing fine. I love my job, I've got my church friends and family, and I've got Jesus in my heart. I know that sounds corny, but I'm happy."

Even though he claimed to be happy, Sarah's heart still broke for him. She knew what it was like to be lonely, and have to readapt to new surroundings and a new circle of friends and neighbors. Even though she'd lived in the suburbs surrounding Vancouver all her life, her parents had moved frequently, forcing her to start again many times. She knew what it was like to be uprooted from everything familiar. Gwen was the only one who had made any effort to keep in touch with her over the years.

Now, as an adult, everyone had busy lives. It was even more difficult to meet new people than ever before. Once out of high school, the only time she met new people was when she changed jobs, which wasn't often. She had a few friends she'd made at the university, but like her, their lives were too busy to expand their social circles beyond the occasional shared lunch.

"I really should get back to work. I can't decide if it's good or bad that nothing happened tonight."

He nodded and patted her hand once again, only this time, he pulled away. "I know what you mean. I hate to have something like this hanging with no direction. But on the other hand, I'm sure whatever is going on is bad. Since there hasn't been anything more *bad* happening, it's good."

Sarah stood. "I have to hurry. I've gone over my fifteen minutes. It's been really good sitting with you. We'll have to do this again."

Matt stood as well. "Yes, or maybe one day we can go someplace else to talk. Like maybe out for dinner on the weekend when we can work out some time between shift work and homework. Anyplace but here."

Suddenly Sarah felt like a schoolgirl being asked out for a first date. She actually felt herself blushing. It was all she could do not to shuffle her feet. "I'd like that," she mumbled. "See you later."

Sarah hurried to the staff room to change back into her

smock and tie her hair up again. Just before she turned the corner, she peeked over her shoulder to see Matt walking out the main door. If she hadn't known who he was, she would never have recognized him from the back without his uniform. Not to say he didn't look good in jeans and a baggy sweatshirt, but she couldn't deny that he looked great in his uniform.

Sarah sighed. Even in normal clothes, Matt Walker was still every inch a cop. Whatever he did, he moved with precision and determination. At the same time, whether he was moving or not, Matt's eyes never kept still unless he was looking directly at her and waiting for an answer to a direct question. He was always watching everything. He seldom moved his head or changed his expression, but he paid attention to everything happening around him and everything that was said, all the time. He remembered it later, too.

She wondered if he did the same thing when he was on a date.

Sarah nearly tripped over her own two feet. She didn't know why she would think about Matt's dating habits. The only reason they were spending time together was because of her discovery. The other times she'd seen him away from the donut shop she had been the one who had gone looking for him. Today was the first time he'd come to see her, only to see what Donnie was up to.

Of course she liked him, and it wasn't simply because he was a cop and in a position of power. When she talked to him as a person, rather than about the situation at the donut shop, she found him warm and fascinating and even a little bit funny.

As soon as Sarah returned to the front counter, Kristie disappeared back into the kitchen to start planning her run of fresh donuts and muffins for the morning rush.

Sarah absently patted the pocket of her smock. Back on the job, she focused her thoughts on work, and forced herself not to wonder what it would be like sitting at a private table with Matt on the weekend. Nothing exciting had happened tonight, and Blair had not shown up. Since the pre-rush hour lineup was due to start soon, she doubted anything would happen today. But if it did, she had Matt's phone number ready, just in case she needed it.

For the rest of her shift, she could relax.

Tomorrow would be another day.

❧

Matt folded his sweatshirt and tucked it into the drawer, then continued to get ready for bed. He couldn't believe he'd worn his disgusting old gym sweatshirt out in public. He'd picked it only because it was so far from his normal dress code, nobody who had seen him out of uniform would recognize him dressed like that. Besides, at such a late hour, no one had really seen him.

Tonight, he'd seen only the ordinary, middle-of-the-night crowd at Donnie's Donuts. The Ronsky boys were their usual loud and obnoxious selves at their usual corner table. Two very inebriated men who'd obviously floated in from the bar down the street had been talking loudly in the center of the room, not caring what they said or who heard them. He'd also seen a small group of young women whom he wouldn't call ladies, talking about their latest escapades in the husband-hunting market.

He hadn't seen the one person he went to see. For the half hour he was there, Donnie hadn't come out of his office. Failing that, he wanted to tell Sarah what to watch for the next time she saw Blair but stopped himself. He couldn't do anything that a defense attorney might, in any way, perceive as coaching. Therefore, instead of describing Blair and asking if his description matched, he had planned to prompt her from the other direction.

Instead of asking if the man had a crooked nose, Matt was going to ask her if Blair's nose was straight. Instead of asking if he had multiple piercings on his left ear, Matt planned to ask about jewelry in general. Instead of asking about the scar on the right side of Blair's chin, Matt planned to ask if the man had any birthmarks or distinguishable features.

Instead of saying anything at all about Blair Kincaid, somehow she got him talking about himself, which he usually didn't do.

No one had ever asked him why he wanted to be a cop. People had asked him what it was like to carry a gun, or what it was like to tell people what to do and have them do it. Or, commonly, people asked him about various law issues and how they could avoid paying for speeding tickets and other infractions. Matt's usual answer to that was to obey the law and not to speed.

Sarah had asked about him, as a person. No one had ever expressed concern that he was alone, away from his family, the people he'd grown up with, and the friends with whom he'd gone to school. Her concern for him as a person touched a part of him he hadn't thought about for a long time.

Maybe she was right. Maybe he was a little bit lonely, but it was of his own choosing. When God found the right woman for him, Matt was sure he would know it. Until that right woman came along, Matt didn't have to stop seeing Sarah; he could still keep seeing her and keep her at a professional distance.

Matt crawled into bed, but he only ended up staring up at the dark ceiling. In not too long, it would be daylight, and he doubted he'd catch any sleep before then. Every time he closed his eyes, he saw a smiling face with enchanting sea green eyes.

seven

"16Bravo4 copy. I'm on my way from 4th and Maynem. ETA. . ." Matt checked the clock on the dashboard. ". . .four minutes. Who else is attending?" As he spoke, he reached forward to turn on the flashing lights and flick the switch to turn the siren on to wail. He quickly checked around for traffic, maneuvered the car into a U-turn, and sped off.

"Closest unit is 10Bravo9 at Oak and United. ETA fifteen minutes."

"16Bravo4 copy." Matt gritted his teeth as he slowed, then steered onto the shoulder and went over the curb to go around someone who remained stopped at a red light, blocking his way at an intersection.

This time, he was responding to a multi-vehicle accident. According to the dispatcher, the possibility of serious injuries was slim. Fortunately, this was the tail end of the second rush hour, and this accident didn't involve a pedestrian. For that, Matt was always grateful. From the sound of things, he would be needed only to direct traffic and collect a few statements. That would see him to approximately 7:00 P.M., when he could sign off, do his reports, go home, and go to bed. With today being the first dayshift of the rotation back to work, he felt as if he was ready to fall down, and no amount of coffee could save him.

As usual, he'd found it hard to sleep the night before. Most members experienced the same patterns on the first twelve-hour shift, and Matt was no different. He was exhausted, partly from the long day, and partly because he hadn't had enough sleep. Instead of relaxing and being able to drift off to sleep, he'd lain awake half the night trying to psyche himself up for the coming four days. In addition to thinking about the investigations he had to finish, Matt also had been thinking about the most important file, one that he hadn't yet started, at least not officially.

He couldn't stop thinking of Sarah, and the possibility of Sarah coming face to face with Blair Kincaid.

Kincaid was a dangerous man, not because he was violent. He was dangerous because he was selfish and ruthless. He allowed nothing, and no one, to stand in his way.

In some ways, Matt had hoped Sarah would call him. He needed to hear her say she hadn't seen anything since he last saw her. Every time the phone rang while he was off duty, he'd checked the time and thought of what Sarah would have been doing. Right now, it was 5:57 P.M. on Wednesday. Sarah would be at home, in bed, where she was safe, sleeping.

As he pulled up to the accident scene and turned off the siren, Matt once again glanced at the time and hit the button for the radio. "16Bravo4."

"16Bravo4," the dispatcher echoed.

"I'm at the scene now. Two cars blocking the intersection, I see people arguing and exchanging information. I'll investigate and advise."

Matt breathed a sigh of relief when he discovered that two of the three vehicles involved were equipped with airbags, and the third car, which wasn't, sustained only minor damage. No ambulance had been called, and he didn't need to call one. This type of MVA, he didn't mind attending.

By the time he finished taking the statements, the other member arrived, which allowed them to direct traffic around the accident. After the tow truck arrived and the debris was cleared, it was time to quit for the day.

"16Bravo4. I'm out of service and on the way in. ETA twenty minutes."

"16Bravo4 copy," the dispatcher's voice echoed back.

After a trip to the works yard to fill up the gas tank, Matt headed for the station. On his way into the building, he waved at a few of the other members from different zones as they were on their way out to the cars. For the next twelve hours, someone else would be 16Bravo4.

He stopped to chat with Ty for a few minutes, then continued on into the general duty area to one of the workstations to finish a few reports that he hadn't completed on the road. Since one of them was needed for a bail hearing the next day, he had to take a little longer than usual, making sure he had all the details accurate. He didn't want some cranky Crown Counselor throwing out his Prosecutors Informant Report as evidence because his handwriting was too sloppy. Or worse, he didn't want to be called at home to come back to redo it because he'd not worded himself clearly.

When all was done, he meandered into the locker room to change. He took the clip out of his gun and stored it in the top drawer, locked it, and slid his revolver into the second drawer, and locked it as well. After he was back in his civvies, he stowed his belt and accessories, then held up his uniform for inspection. Unfortunately, he'd picked up some mud at the last MVA, requiring a trip to the dry cleaners.

He closed his locker and set the lock, and, finally, Matt was on his way home.

The first thing he did when he stepped in the door of his townhouse was check his answering machine. The flashing red light showed two calls. He waited impatiently through the first message, which was from the worship leader asking to schedule a date when he could play guitar for a solo, then suggesting a number of possibilities. Matt held his breath while he waited for the machine to start on the second call. Part of him hoped it was Sarah, yet at the same time, he dreaded the possibility. If she called, the only reason would be that something bad had happened.

Instead of Sarah's sweet, melodic voice, all he heard was a click, followed by dial tone.

As Matt sighed, the deep intake of breath was all it took to induce a massive yawn. Being alone, he didn't bother to stifle it or cover his mouth. He hit the rewind button, picked up the remote, and turned on the television. He knew he'd missed the news, but having the television on would be background noise while he wound down to get ready for bed. The second day shift was always better than the first. Even though he had to get up at 5:30 A.M. to be at the station for the 6:30 debriefing, he was so tired, he knew that once his head hit the pillow, he'd sleep like a log.

Tomorrow would be another day. For this rotation, his first night shift was Friday night. It bugged him when he didn't have time to take breaks on Friday night shifts, but this time, he didn't care. Sarah didn't work Friday nights, so if he didn't make it to the donut shop, it was no big deal.

⋙

Every time the glass door opened, Sarah struggled not to look like she was checking to see who had just entered. Of course, she knew she wouldn't see Matt. It was a new week and a new rotation. Matt would be in bed sleeping, having finished his first day shift. A couple of officers had come in earlier, this time a man and a woman. Sarah always liked the police to come in, because, except for the Ronsky clan, their presence usually kept the riffraff out. Over the past year since she'd started working at the donut shop, she'd probably met every single member of the local RCMP detachment.

After the two officers left, Donnie's cell phone beeped its unique song.

Sarah's stomach lurched. While not every call Donnie got on his cell phone would be ominous, she'd already seen that when it rang minutes after the police left, it usually meant only one thing, especially in the middle of the night.

Donnie unclipped the phone from his belt and hit the button. He checked his watch, nodded, and said only the word "yes." He disappeared into his office with the phone still next to his ear and closed the door. Five minutes later, he reappeared, but he didn't go into the kitchen or take over at the front counter to give Kristie or herself a break. Instead, Donnie began fiddling with the latté machine, which Sarah knew was recently filled because she'd done it herself less than an hour ago.

Not even five minutes passed before the door opened, and the man named Blair walked in. Sarah made a mental note that the time was 3:48 A.M. Because Matt needed a description of this man, Sarah quickly looked into his face. While counting to five, so she wouldn't be caught looking too long, she tried to memorize everything she could about him before she turned around.

Trying to appear discreet, Sarah dropped a napkin and some crumbs onto the floor. She turned around and forced herself to walk slowly to the closet. Since Kristie was busy at the counter trying to help the Ronsky clan decide what variety of chocolate donuts they wanted, Sarah was able to slip into the closet without being seen. Without turning on the light, she shut the door quietly behind her.

In an instant, she dropped to her knees and crawled as close as she could to the vent.

Donnie was sitting at his desk. He punched some numbers into his calculator, then turned it so Blair, who was standing in front of him, could see the total. When Donnie spoke, his voice was so hushed Sarah had to strain to hear. "This is what I'm expecting from this batch."

Blair hit a few numbers and turned the calculator back to Donnie. "Less your purchase, of course."

"Of course."

"How much time do you need? I told Lennie a week."

"A week is fine. Can I count this?"

"Count it if you want. I've got all the time in the world."

"I'll just make a quick check while you're here." As Donnie reached into the open briefcase, Sarah's heart stopped, then started up in double time. Finally, she would learn the answer to the mystery of the contents, so valuable the briefcase was locked into the safe every time it appeared.

Donnie lifted out a small bundle. He flipped through it, nodded, and laid it on the desk. "Everything appears to be in order."

Sarah held her breath.

Money. And lots of it. She could see from the colors that the denominations were high.

She didn't need to hear the rest of the conversation. She shuffled backward instead of rising to her feet in order to make the least amount of noise. When she came to the door, she rose, grabbed the broom and dustpan, wrapped her hand around the doorknob and froze.

If either Blair or Donnie saw her with the broom, they would know she had been in the closet.

She didn't know if Donnie knew his office was so accessible from the closet, but she couldn't take the chance.

Sarah tucked the broom and dustpan back into place, opened the door a crack, and peeked out. Not seeing Kristie, she slipped out and gently pressed the door closed behind her.

The urge to run back into the restaurant area was so strong she had to force herself to walk in a leisurely pace. Kristie was still not so patiently serving one of the Ronskys, so Sarah avoided making eye contact while she opened the gate between the counter and the restaurant. As quickly as she could without running, Sarah returned to the table she'd been cleaning when Blair walked in and resumed her chore.

She purposely kept her back to the door of Donnie's office, but the click of the lock and the whoosh of the door opening gonged like a cymbal in her head. In order to keep her back turned, she returned the plates to the table and crouched down to pick up the napkin she'd dropped earlier. When she heard the main door open and close again, she scooped everything up, kicked the crumbs under the table, and returned to the kitchen.

She noticed that Donnie's door was again closed.

Matt's words about Donnie usually leaving his door ajar a few inches echoed in her head.

She knew why the door was closed. She didn't even doubt that the door was locked.

The king was in his counting house, counting all his money.

Sarah shook her head. She'd never been so scared in her life, and she was about to start reciting nursery rhymes.

She had no idea of the amount of money involved, but she'd heard the sound of the one full briefcase as it landed on the desk. The dull thud confirmed that it was close to full, meaning the amount of money it contained would likely be staggering.

Her heart pounded in her chest as she checked her watch. She had to phone Matt. He told her to wake him up if something happened. However, this was not a call she could make on the company phone. Either Kristie or Donnie could pick up the line at any time and hear her conversation. She couldn't take the risk.

She thought of borrowing Kristie's cell phone, but she didn't know where in the small building she could go to make a private call. Even if she went into the staff room and closed the door, she couldn't be assured no one would walk in or overhear. Besides, it was too odd for her to be making a phone call in the middle of the night. She'd never made a personal call on company time. No one she knew was awake at such hours. She couldn't make a personal call without raising Donnie's interest.

Fortunately, the morning rush was starting, which gave Sarah something else to think about. Still, the problem never left her mind as she tried to sort it out enough to tell Matt.

At the end of her shift, Sarah usually went straight to the university for her first class. Today, she made a detour into the police station. By this time, Matt had started his shift and would be out on the road. Even so, she thought he'd get the message sooner than if she left a message on his answering machine at home.

She barely made it to the university in time to find a parking spot and run into her class before the bell rang.

All morning she was distracted and struggled to concentrate on the learning curves for different ages, instead of trying to calculate how much money could possibly have been in the briefcase.

She'd worked herself into a tizzy by the time she arrived at her apartment. She didn't know what she was going to do until after 7:00 P.M., the end of Matt's shift. The only thing she did know was that she wouldn't be able to sleep. Sleep was hard enough on a normal day when the world and all her neighbors were busy and living their lives. She usually went to bed mid-afternoon in order to get enough sleep to last her through the night shift, although it was harder to sleep some days than others.

She had made herself a pot of tea and just settled down at the table when the buzzer for the downstairs' door sounded.

Sarah's heart caught in her throat. Everyone she knew except Gwen was at work. Gwen would never come over without phoning first, especially at this hour. Gwen respected that Sarah would normally be starting to get ready for bed even though it was the middle of the day. Besides, Gwen had her baby to take care of. Therefore it wouldn't be Gwen.

She wasn't expecting a delivery.

She wasn't expecting anyone or anything.

A sinking feeling of dread flowed though Sarah, making her knees weak. If Donnie knew that she'd seen something, he wouldn't confront her at the donut shop in front of Kristie. He would talk to her when no one was watching. He could easily get her address from her personnel file.

Sarah's stomach stared to roll. Donnie had a gun. She'd seen it. Very possibly, if Donnie were here, he'd have the gun in his pocket. . .

The buzzer sounded again.

Instead of picking up the phone, Sarah ran through the living room and onto her balcony. She peered down from the safety of the sixth floor, looking to see if Donnie's car was in the visitor parking. If she saw his car, she could run down the stairs and out the back door.

The visitor parking spaces were empty.

But there was a police car parked in front of the building, in the no-parking zone.

eight

Matt pushed the buzzer for Sarah's apartment a third time then checked his watch. He had hoped to arrive early enough that she wouldn't already be sleeping, but apparently, he'd been wrong. Still, even knowing she was sleeping, he didn't have a choice. The only reason she would have left a message at the station for him to call would be because she'd seen something she considered important, even urgent.

The second he got her message, he'd sent a question out on the radio to ask what the word was on Kincaid and his current dealings. He'd received many private answers on the computer, plus he'd brought the topic up at a recent debriefing. He didn't like the answer.

Not only was Kincaid out of jail, he was definitely back in active "duty" on the streets. Only this time, he'd gotten smarter. Short of a twenty-four-hour surveillance, they couldn't determine exactly what he was doing or with whom he was dealing. They only knew that Blair Kincaid was up to no good because suddenly he had money and, as usual, no job to go with it.

Finally, Sarah's voice blared through the speaker. "Matt! Come right up!" The buzzer sounded.

He opened his mouth, almost saying his usual "16Bravo4 copy" but he caught himself. He smiled and pulled the door open.

As he walked through the lobby to the elevator, a man and a woman appeared from the hallway. Their eyes widened, and they slowed their pace to watch Matt as he continued walking toward the elevator. Knowing they were watching, Matt reached up to touch the brim of his hat and gave them a smile and a brief nod. They gave him a nervous smile in return, then walked faster until they were behind Matt, and he couldn't see them anymore.

Matt pushed the button for the elevator and waited, not turning around while the couple exited the building.

He'd been an RCMP member for eight years. After all that time he should have been used to people staring at him, but sometimes it still bothered him. He knew he was intruding on those people's homes by being in their apartment block, but he wasn't the bad guy. He was an officer of the law. It was his job to help people. He told himself the reason these people were staring was because, in their minds, seeing him inside their building could only mean that something was wrong.

In a way, they were right. Something was wrong. Blair Kincaid was back on the streets. Maybe not in their neighborhood, but he was definitely back. The key to getting him off the streets and back into jail, unfortunately, lay with Sarah.

Once inside the elevator, Matt watched the lights above the door change as he ascended to the sixth floor. As the door opened, Sarah became visible inch by inch. He had barely taken his first step out of the elevator, when she launched herself at him. Instinctively, his hand wrapped around the handle of his gun while Sarah's arms wrapped around him.

"Matt! I'm so glad you're here! I'm so scared!"

Matt didn't move as the elevator door swooshed closed behind him. Very slowly, he relaxed his grip on the gun. Even more slowly, he moved his hands to Sarah's back. Instead of relaxing once his arms were around her, she tightened her grip on him.

He couldn't help himself. Even though he was on duty, and even though Sarah was a potential witness and informant, he moved his arms, shuffled his feet, and embraced her fully.

She fit just right in his arms, and it felt good to hold her. She was soft and warm, and the steadfastness of her grip around his back told him that she needed him.

It had been a long time since he felt needed by any one peson in particular. The force needed him, but he was just one of many uniforms following the strict code of law enforcement rules to preserve right versus wrong and help the good guy win once in a while.

But Sarah didn't want just any officer. She wanted him. She could have told her story to anyone at the station; he'd even told her to do so if the shift work made seeing him difficult when something finally broke. Instead, she'd left the message only for him.

He had to admit that in the short time since they'd started talking he'd become quite fond of her. When they had parted in the parking lot of the restaurant after church on Sunday, he'd wanted to do exactly what he was doing right now, which was to hold her in his arms and not let go.

Matt squeezed his eyes shut. He wanted to kiss her, but he couldn't. For this moment, he was in uniform, on duty. He was to be Sarah's protector, and nothing else.

In his early days as a cop, he had struggled with the power of the uniform. He was not unique. Just being a cop gave him the authority to make people obey whatever he said, whether he had earned the respect deserving of the uniform or not. In the locker room, the allure of the uniform to women in general was a hot topic of conversation, especially among the newer members of the force, unless, of course, those women were other officers.

But Sarah had been with him out of uniform, and as far as he could tell, she liked him anyway. Now that he was back in uniform and on duty, he was supposed to keep an impersonal distance. He certainly shouldn't have been holding a witness, but he couldn't help it.

Matt lowered his head and brushed his cheek against the hair on top of her head. In the back of his mind, he logged that since he was wearing his boots, and she was only in her socks, there was a greater height difference than normal. It made her feel smaller than she really was, which only magnified the feeling of protectiveness he felt toward her.

He wanted to make her happy—to tell her everything was okay now, but he couldn't lie. He couldn't tell her she was now safe just because he was there. Nor could he say everything would be all right. His gut tightened, knowing he had to be realistic. Unless she had some very specific information, they didn't even know what they were dealing with or really even whom. In the major scheme of things, as bad as he was, Blair Kincaid was just a little cog in a very big wheel.

"Maybe we should get out of the hallway. Let's go inside your apartment, so we can talk."

When she backed up, her cheeks turned a most charming shade of pink. "You're right. I'm sorry. This way."

Sarah's apartment was much like he imagined it would be. Being Thursday, and knowing her busy schedule, he could understand why it was so messy, especially since he knew she wasn't expecting him. He didn't know whether or not to be amused that she made no apologies as she guided him through the kitchen, strewn with unwashed dishes, and into the living room. She picked up a couple of books, a notepad, and a pen off the couch, then refolded a newspaper that was spread all over the coffee table and picked it up as well. She rammed the pile into an already overstuffed magazine pouch on the floor and motioned for him to sit down.

Mess aside, the apartment was small and very utilitarian. The furniture was sparse, but appeared comfortable and practical, once he could see it.

He sat on one end of the couch, and Sarah sat on the other. He pulled his notepad out of his pocket. "Did something happen last night?"

She nodded so fast her hair bounced. "He came in again. He's got this really ugly nose, with a bump right here." She pressed one finger to the bridge of her own nose, not moving her finger when she continued. "I guess he's about 35, but he could be younger and just look older because he's ugly. I didn't see what color his eyes were, but his hair is cut real short all around. It's a kind of nondescript dark brown, no grey, and it's all the same length—like it's been shaved and he's growing it back. His hairline is kind of receding, but I couldn't see if he had a bald spot on top and he's got like five earrings on his ear." Her finger moved from her nose to her left ear. "He also has a birthmark on his cheek and a totally ugly scar on his chin."

She switched hands and used the index finger of her right hand to draw a straight line on the side of her chin, exactly matching the scar Blair Kincaid obtained from his last knife altercation. "And he's five-foot-ten-and-a-half in his shoes. When he came through the door, I saw where his head came up to on the poster they put beside the door. When Donnie was in the bathroom, I measured it."

Matt jotted everything down, even though he knew the answers before she said them. There was no doubt in his mind the guy she was describing. He could especially confirm the ugly part, because Blair Kincaid was ugly from the inside out.

He closed the notepad. "That's a great description." He stood and grinned, trying to quell the anxiety that had begun to eat at his stomach now that what he had dreaded was confirmed. "Good work, Detective Cunningham."

The second her name left his mouth, he mentally kicked himself. She hadn't told him her last name. The only reason he knew was because he'd called up her personal information from her license plate number. Technically, he wasn't supposed to know her address, either. All she'd ever given him was her phone number. The only thing he was officially supposed to know was her first name from her tag at the donut shop.

She didn't seem to notice. Sarah also jumped to her feet. "Wait! There's more! I know what is in those briefcases he brings in."

Matt's heart started beating faster, but he didn't move. "Go on."

She sank back down to the couch, so Matt did too.

"Money. Lots of money. He brought another one today. I don't know how much it was, but that briefcase was completely full. So was the first one, because I heard the sound of the first one as it hit the desk, and it was stuffed. This morning when Blair came in with another briefcase, it took Donnie over half an hour to count it, there was that much. I don't know it's the same briefcase going back and forth, but if there's more than one, they're identical. I've seen three so far come in, but I never see any going out. Do you have any idea what's going on?"

"Not for sure. We only know that Kincaid is up to something. He's already been under suspicion for a while. We just haven't caught him yet. Then, once we figure out what he's doing, we have to gather evidence to make an arrest and get a conviction. Just catching him with a suitcase of money is mighty suspicious, but unless we know how and where he got it, there's nothing we can do."

Sarah's voice lowered, and she leaned toward him. "I'll bet they're laundering money."

Matt made a few more notes, then tucked the pad back into his pocket. "That would be my guess too. I'll have to make out a report and forward it to my shift NCO, and we'll take it from there. From Kincaid's history, it looks like it would be drug money, and Donnie's laundering it. This is going to be quite an investigation."

"How long do you think it will take before you can arrest that Kincaid guy?"

"I can't answer that until I know what we're dealing with."

Matt should have stood, but he couldn't move. He sat on the couch, transfixed by Sarah's enchanting sea green eyes. She was staring at him, watching, waiting for him to say something, although he didn't know what.

Her voice dropped even lower, in both pitch and volume. "What about Donnie?"

Matt straightened. "I don't know. It looks like he's the one actually laundering the money, so he's obviously going to be arrested. But with Blair Kincaid involved, there's a much bigger picture. We're going to leave them alone and see what develops, and then arrest everyone involved at once."

"If Donnie's arrested and thrown in jail, what will happen to the donut shop? What about my job? And everybody else who works there?"

Matt cleared his throat. "If he's convicted for laundering money, under the criminal code all assets that can be proven to be obtained by illegal earnings are seized. The taxation department jumps on these things pretty quick, as that's money that can be made for the taxpayer. The business could be bought by someone else, after the fees and legal bills are paid, which would be a lot after it goes to trial. If no one buys it, then it just closes down, and the government takes what is owed. If there's anything left by then."

His heart constricted as Sarah slumped and buried her face in her hands. "It's bad enough that I've been spying on my boss. But if the business is suddenly shut down, what am I going to do? I'll never get another job that will give me the hours I need to keep going to school. It was hard enough to find this one. I can't survive without a job. I need something to live on while I go to school."

"These things don't happen overnight. Sometimes investigations take months. Sometimes the big ones go on for over a year."

She raised her head. "And sometimes they happen in days."

"I don't think that's going to happen this time. Not with the amount of money it appears we're dealing with."

Her face paled. "Am I going to get fingered?"

"Fingered?"

"If they find out I'm the one supplying this information, am I going to get bumped off? You know. Like, cement overshoes?"

"This isn't an old gangster movie, Sarah. People call in tips like this all the time. It's not as if you're directly involved in the middle of things and you're the only person who could know what is going on. If you're careful and don't show that you know anything, when they get busted, they'll just chalk it up to another sterling RCMP investigation. As I said, we've already got Kincaid under suspicion. And this time, I'm going to get him. All of him."

Her eyes widened. Matt should have left at that moment, but he couldn't have moved if he wanted to.

"That sounded personal."

He cleared his throat. "I shouldn't have said that. I'm not in a position to talk about it."

"It's okay. I understand."

He patted the pocket with the note pad in it. "You do realize that even if you've changed your mind about how far you want to go with this, I have to report everything you've said. You can request to remain anonymous for the purpose of further investigation, but I have to put your name on the report as a complainant, or else we're back to square one."

She was silent for a very long minute. She gulped. "I know. I guess I didn't think this the whole way through—or what would happen after I found out what was going on and all that. I don't even know what's really going on. Only that there's lots of money involved."

Matt finally stood. They walked in silence to the door. Matt removed his hat and turned around before opening the door and walking into the hallway. "I guess I won't see you on my break tomorrow."

"No. Tonight is my last night to work. For you, the wee hours after midnight is still Thursday night, but for me, since I start at midnight, it's the start of my day Friday. I get off work when everyone else is starting their day. Most people don't understand how that works."

He nodded. "Working odd hours can be very confusing to someone who has only worked nine to five." He paused. While he didn't talk, he rotated the hat in his hands by the brim. If nothing else urgent came up, he wouldn't see her until his next nightshift coffee break that happened between Sunday night and Thursday night. He'd counted ahead on his calendar, and that wasn't going to happen again for two weeks.

While he knew he shouldn't have been pursuing a relationship with a non-Christian, she had been to church twice.

While he hoped she was drawing closer to God, he didn't know where she was, and as such, he wasn't going to date her. But they could at least be friends. When off-duty, of course.

"Can I see you tomorrow afternoon? You'll be finished with classes at noon, right? I don't have to be at the station for debriefing until six-thirty at night. It's a strange transition for me, switching between days and nights in one day. I usually sleep for a few hours to make it a regular night after working days, but I get up really early so I can go back to bed about three in the afternoon and grab a few hours of sleep before starting the next twelve-hour shift at 7:00 P.M."

She smiled. Something in Matt's stomach went haywire, telling him he probably should have had lunch.

"You know, I understand that. Would you like to go out for lunch? We just have to make sure we don't go too late, so you can get a decent sleep before you have to go to work."

He continued to rotate the hat in his hands. "Sounds good. Want me to pick you up? I always go to the gym between day and night shift. It helps to tire me out so I can sleep in the middle of the day." He set the hat back on his head and patted his stomach with one hand. "I've got to keep in shape. Some days I sit too much, driving around all the time."

Matt forced himself to hold back a smile when she looked down to his stomach, blushed, then quickly returned her gaze to his face.

"I'll be coming from the university, so how about if we just meet somewhere?"

He didn't always want to meet her, then go their separate ways from a parking lot. It may have been old-fashioned of him, but Matt wanted to be able to pick her up and return her to her door. But, as they both knew the hard way, shift work had a way of taking a toll on a person's life. "I guess that would work," he muttered.

They chose a restaurant halfway between the university and the gym and picked a time.

When he wrapped his hand around the doorknob, before he

had time to pull the door open, Sarah's tiny hand covered his.

"Before you go, I want to thank you for coming to talk to me. I was really scared, and even though nothing's changed, by your coming now and not waiting until tonight, you've made me feel a lot better. Mostly, thanks for being honest with me about what could possibly happen. At least I know what to expect, and I can get ready for it."

"No problem. I should be the one thanking you for doing the right thing. Not everyone would stick their neck out like this."

"Well. . .anyway. . ." She lifted her hand. "I guess I'll see you tomorrow."

"Yeah," he mumbled and made his way out.

All the way to the car, Matt felt incomplete, like there was something he hadn't wrapped up properly. The trouble was, he knew exactly what he hadn't done.

He shouldn't have felt this way, and he certainly didn't have the right to do so, but he had wanted to kiss her goodbye.

"16Bravo4. Back in service," he said to the radio as he settled into the car and prepared to drive away.

"16Bravo4," echoed the dispatcher. "Disturbance at Mayfair Park, east entrance, 5th and Pineridge. A male juvenile hit a parked car with a bike. No injuries, but the motorist has seized the bike. The juvenile isn't very happy. Witness reporting says threats have been issued. You're first responder."

Matt reached forward to turn on the flashing lights and sped off. "16Bravo4 copy," he muttered, then turned the siren on to wail.

If there were anything he could appreciate about the job, it was that no two days were the same.

nine

Sarah looked around as she walked into the big building. Matt had just come off two night shifts. For him, working a twelve-hour shift meant Saturday night stretched into Sunday morning. So being Saturday night, she knew he seldom got off on time, on what was typically the busiest night shift of the week. Therefore, he never knew if he would be at church when his rotation fell that way. He'd said that there were times that he was still working or filling in reports at ten o'clock when church was starting, even though he was "supposed" to get off at seven. Or, if he did get off, he was typically exhausted after working all night, so the alternate was that he would be passed out in bed.

Since she didn't immediately see him, she hoped he was sleeping because she certainly hoped he wasn't still working.

Therefore, today she was alone. She couldn't even sit with Gwen and Lionel because they were still away on vacation. But that was okay.

For the first time in her life, Sarah wanted to come to church, even if she had to sit alone. For the past two weeks, the pastor's message about God loving people who made bad decisions had been fascinating. At first she'd felt very safe about going to heaven, since the Bible talked about these people having committed major sins like murder and adultery. She'd never killed anyone, and she wasn't married, so she couldn't commit adultery. She led a good life, and she was basically a good person.

But at the tail end of last week's sermon, the pastor had talked about other sins that weren't so bad. Lying. Cheating. Even speeding or rolling through a stop sign. Most of the people in the congregation had responded with a nervous laugh about that—everyone except Matt. He gave people tickets for those sins. She hadn't felt bad until the pastor pointed out that heaven was only for those who were as perfect as God, which meant no sins at all, not even the little ones.

Sarah figured she led a pretty good life, but she certainly wasn't as perfect as God. In their conversation on Friday, before Matt started his first night shift, he'd mentioned that even though he might face death in the line of duty, he didn't fear dying.

Matt was a good man. Matt was even a wonderful man. But he wasn't as perfect as God. Yet he said he knew he was going to heaven, without a doubt.

Today, she wanted to hear more. In fact, she thought she'd pay attention better if she didn't have Matt sitting beside her.

On her journey into the sanctuary, a few people she'd met before welcomed her. Sarah felt good that they recognized her. She chatted for a few minutes then continued on her way. She settled into a corner seat and followed the order of the service just as she had when Matt had been with her. This time, she was a little more familiar with the routine. She could even sing along with two of the songs, which helped ease the feeling of being a stranger. As expected, the pastor's sermon had her nearly riveted on the edge of her seat as he spoke about how salvation was for everyone who simply believed.

The sermon ended before he could explain exactly what it meant to believe.

And that meant only one thing. Sarah knew she would be back again next week.

A few more people whom she'd met when she was with Matt greeted her on the way out. She even stopped to talk to someone in the parking lot who recognized her from the donut shop, which was a pleasant surprise.

Her tummy rumbled at the same time as the motor of her car roared to a start, making Sarah smile. With the graphic reminder, Sarah drove straight home, intending to make a quick lunch with whatever she had on hand. However, one look at the kitchen stopped her dead in her tracks.

All weekend long, instead of catching up on her housework, she'd been frantically catching up on her homework. For the first time in months, after studying and writing all weekend, she was now ahead on her assignments. Before she realized the state of the rest of her apartment, she thought she could relax. However, she couldn't do that—she couldn't even eat until she at least found room on the counter to make herself a sandwich.

Mentally kicking herself, Sarah grabbed an apple to munch. She ate it while she cleaned up the backlog of dirty dishes and scrubbed the counter and sink clean. She was halfway through washing the floor when the phone rang.

A low and very pleasant voice drifted over the line. "Hi, Sarah."

"Matt? What are you doing awake? What time did you get to bed?"

"I only had to stay an hour late this morning, so I fell asleep about nine."

Sarah looked at the clock and counted on her fingers. "It's one now. That means you've had only four hours sleep."

She could hear the smile in his voice. "I've gotten by with less. Besides, I don't want to sleep all day. What are you doing? Want to do it together?"

Sarah glanced into the living room. It was fairly clean. The biggest mess was her papers strewn about the coffee table, and her current textbook open and face down on the arm of the couch, which seemed to be its permanent place unless she was in class.

With her apartment now tidied up, she should have gone back to her reading, but she'd done enough work for the weekend. For months, all she'd done was work, homework, and housework. She deserved a break.

She smiled into the phone as she spoke. "I didn't really want to do homework today, anyway. If you're tired, why don't you come here, and I'll make you some nice, fresh coffee."

"I'd like that. ETA twenty-two minutes. Bye."

Sarah smiled as she hung up the phone and walked into the kitchen. Matt wasn't as awake as he thought he was. He may have been at home, but his brain was still half-functioning in cop mode. For that reason, Sarah put an extra scoop of coffee into the machine.

Before he arrived, she finished washing the kitchen floor, then ran around the living room to pick up whatever she could to make it presentable.

The buzzer for the downstairs door went off at the twenty-one-minute mark, giving her just enough time to kick a sock under the couch and ram her homework into the magazine rack.

When she opened the door to let Matt into her apartment, she could see that, just as she suspected, he definitely wasn't as awake as he claimed to be. Dark circles shadowed his eyes, and for the first time since she'd met him, his posture wasn't perfect military-upright. Yet, just as he had been at church, he was dressed as neat as a pin. He wore fairly new jeans that were spotlessly clean and a nicely pressed, green short-sleeved shirt.

"Hi. That coffee smells good."

Sarah grinned as she poured two cups, very glad that she'd started her cleaning spree before she knew he was coming. "I know you're tired, but I would think when you drink so much coffee every day when you work, you wouldn't touch it on your days off."

"One can never have too much coffee."

They sat in the clean living room together, on opposite ends of the couch, sipping coffee in silence. While she'd already learned that Matt tended to be more of a listener than a speaker, Sarah thought today that he was quieter than usual.

"How was your night? Anything exciting or just average?"

He made a very humorless laugh. "There's no such thing as average. Some things are predictable, like parties and more drunk driving accidents on the weekends, but really, no two days or nights are alike."

"Tell me about last night, then, as un-average as it was."

Not that she expected a rundown of his whole thirteen-hour shift, but when a long silence hung between them, Sarah suddenly wondered if perhaps she shouldn't have asked. She knew some of the things he did were confidential, and she now worried that her question was out of line. He'd told her a few of the funny things that happened, like the time a woman thought she had a burglar trapped in the basement. It ended up being a bird that had somehow flown into the house. But she also knew not everything was like that, and many of the things they laughed about were only funny the next day.

She opened her mouth to tell him it was okay, that he didn't have to tell her, but when she turned to look at him, her words caught in her throat.

Matt slouched forward until his elbows rested in the middle of his thighs. He cradled the mug between both his hands. With his head down, he stared intently into the cup, not looking at her or anything else in the room. As he spoke, his voice skipped. "I attended a really bad MVA last night. A drunk driver crossed the center line. Ran head-on into another car. They called me as first responder."

He turned the cup, almost as if he were studying the picture on the side, but he didn't sit upright. Instead, he sighed, then took a long sip from his slouched position and turned all his attention to the contents of the cup as he again cradled it between his palms.

"The other car was a midsized late model. It was a woman and a young boy, about ten or eleven. She must not have been wearing a seat belt because she was thrown clear. It was 5:07 A.M., so not many people were out at that hour on a Sunday morning. When I got there, two people were standing over a woman lying on the road. But I heard crying coming from the car, so I went to the car first. The boy was still seat-belted in the front seat. He was badly hurt. The car was completely crushed. I radioed for a Jaws of Life to come."

He took another sip of his coffee.

"He was crying. He was pinned, so I couldn't have moved him even if I had tried. All I could do was hold his hand. He asked if his mommy was hurt, and I told her that she was. He

looked up at me with his battered little face and said 'Tell my
mommy I love her.' And then he died. Right there while I was
holding his hand. I was kinda shook up, but I wanted to honor
his last request. So I went to where she was laying on the
ground, but she was already dead." His voice skipped. "I was
too late to tell that woman her little boy loved her."

"Oh. . .Matt. . .I'm so sorry. . . ."

He set the mug on the coffee table, and with his elbows still
resting on his knees, Matt lowered his face into his palms. "This
morning, the sound of kids playing outside woke me up," he muttered through his fingers. His voice skipped again. "Listening to
the laughing and screaming, I could only think of that little boy
who loved his mommy, who will never laugh and play again."

His shoulders heaved. Even though the sound was muffled
from his face being covered by his hands, Sarah thought she
heard a sniffle.

Just watching him, her heart broke—for the unknown people
who had lost their lives and for Matt, the big strong cop with a
heart of gold.

She set her cup on the coffee table, shuffled down the couch,
rested one palm on his back, and rubbed gently. "I wish there
was something I could say or do. Would a hug help?"

Without a word, Matt dropped his hands from his face,
turned, and wrapped his arms around her. He'd moved quickly,
and for the most part, he'd kept his head down. In the split
second she saw his face, Sarah had seen that his eyes were red
and, watery and one cheek glistened. He nestled his head in
the crook of her shoulder and held on tight.

Slowly, she wrapped both her arms around him and held
him just as tight as he held her. His breathing was ragged, so
she just held him and rubbed little circles on his back with one
hand, without talking, to give him the time he needed.

After having to handle such a thing, she could see why he had
trouble sleeping, and especially why he couldn't go back to sleep,
with the sounds of the children playing outside on a warm,

sunny, Sunday afternoon. She couldn't imagine the pain of being in that kind of situation. Sarah found it difficult when one of her fish died. She didn't know what she would do if she found herself in the same spot with a person, especially a child.

The more she thought about the life he led, the more she realized she couldn't handle the things he came face-to-face with every day. She'd panicked and fallen apart and let her imagination run away with her after simply witnessing money being exchanged. In order to handle all the various trials and tribulations of law enforcement officers, they would have to be able to build a wall around themselves as a shield against the world. Yet at the same time, they had to be able to handle those situations in the middle of the worst of it, and still be able to help those same people. She didn't know how they did it.

When Matt's breathing settled back into a regular pattern, Sarah stopped moving her hand. "Tell you what. Why don't you come into the kitchen with me? I really haven't had anything to eat today, and I doubt you have either. We can make supper together, and since you're going to help make it, you can help eat it too."

As Matt released his grip around her back, Sarah did the same. He straightened, swiped one hand over his face, and looked straight at her, unashamed of his red eyes.

"Keeping busy sounds like a good idea. I'm not handling this very well. We're supposed to be able to distance ourselves and maintain an emotional barrier, but sometimes it's really hard."

"It's okay. I understand. I really do."

Sarah stood, and Matt did likewise. He followed her into the kitchen and waited behind her while she dug everything she needed for her favorite beef tamale casserole out of the fridge. Most Sundays, she made herself a large casserole. Then, over the next few days, she would eat a little bit each day when she got home from class at noon. That would be her supper, or whatever anyone who worked odd shifts called a full meal at lunchtime, which was the end of her day. Typically, she would eat a sandwich during the break that she called lunch just before the working world started coming through the drive-thru at 5:30 A.M. to get their breakfast. She didn't know what she called breakfast, unless that was the little snack she wolfed down at 11:30 P.M. after she woke up and ran out the door so she wouldn't be late for the start of her shift at midnight.

She didn't want to think of Matt's schedule. At least she worked the same schedule all the time. His changing from days to nights to a longer stretch off in the middle, then back to days again would probably drive most people crazy.

As they worked together, they filled their time with meaningless banter and light conversation. By the time Matt actually laughed at something she said, the sound was like music to her ears.

When everything was complete and the casserole was in the oven, they returned to the living room, where they continued to joke around and even throw pillows at each other until the timer went off.

Sarah placed the whole casserole dish in the center of the table and waited for Matt to help himself first, since he was company. Instead, he folded his hands in front of him and smiled at her. "Before we eat, can we pause for a word of thanks? I have to be honest with you. When we went out to the restaurant, I didn't suggest it because I didn't know how you felt about that, especially in a public place. But now that we've come to know each other a little better, I think this would be a good start, to pray together."

Sarah felt her cheeks heat up. She should have known he would be accustomed to praying before supper. Whenever she was with Gwen, Gwen always prayed before they ate. She also knew that Gwen prayed at restaurants, because Gwen always closed her eyes and paused for a few seconds before she ate. Come to think of it, all three times she'd been out with Matt, he'd done the same as Gwen.

"I guess," she mumbled.

He smiled and bowed his head, leaving his hands, which were

already folded together, on top of the table in front of him. "Dear Heavenly Father, I thank You for this meal we're about to share. Thank You for Your love and all the provisions You give us, and I ask that You bless this time together. Amen."

"Amen," she mumbled.

Sarah helped herself to the salad she'd managed to throw together, while Matt went straight for the casserole. She tried not to stare at the amount he heaped onto his plate, thinking that it would take her two days to eat what he had taken for one. But then, Matt was a large man, much larger than the last man she'd dated.

She nearly dropped her fork at the thought.

She wasn't dating Matt. As much as she liked him, she didn't intend to date him either.

Today she'd seen a small sample of what he went through as a cop, and it made her think of what else he did from day to day. One of those things was handling criminals. And criminals were dangerous. As sweet as Matt was, he obviously had a side she didn't see because, in order to survive, he had to be just as rough and mean as the criminals he combated.

"This is really good. I'm not much of a cook, but it seemed pretty easy to make. Can I have your recipe?"

All she could do was stare at him. He was a cop. A tough guy. "You cook?"

He grinned. "I gotta eat, so that means I gotta cook. No one else does it for me, and I can't live on take-out."

"I guess. . ."

She scrounged around the kitchen for a pen and paper and wrote out the recipe, which she'd made so many times she had it memorized. While she wrote, Matt helped himself to more of her casserole. "I really like this stuff."

"I could never tell."

"You know, if I doubled the recipe, I bet it would last for a couple of days."

Sarah studied her nearly empty casserole dish, which now only contained enough for a bedtime snack. "You sure about that?"

"Yeah. If I made a salad or something. That was a good idea. I never make salads. I guess it's not a guy thing."

He stood and tucked the recipe in his back pocket. Without asking first, he stacked the dishes, gathered the cutlery and glasses, and carried them to the sink.

"What are you doing?"

"The dishes. Your kitchen looked so nice and tidy when I got here, I'd like to leave it in the same condition I first saw it."

She almost told him that he was a guest, and therefore shouldn't be in her kitchen, but she stopped herself short. She had struggled to clean up, and she appreciated the help to get it clean once again more than she cared to admit.

"Before we start, let me put the casserole dish in the sink to soak for a few minutes. You go turn on the television, and I'll be right with you."

He turned and walked into the living room. Sarah couldn't believe how much of the doorway he filled on his way through. Even from the back, he was gorgeous—tall, with broad shoulders, yet trim and physically fit. Not only did he look good in his uniform, he also looked good in casual clothes.

She turned and buried her face in her hands at her wayward thoughts. The man was a police officer. It was probably disrespectful to think that way about him, especially after what he'd just been through.

The television clicked on. A few channels flipped by, stopping on an episode of classic Star Trek. Knowing that he was occupied, Sarah dug her cookbook out of the cupboard. While he was watching television, she intended to surprise him by finding another recipe or two that he could make for himself, since he had been so impressed with her simple dinner.

She wrote out three others that she'd tried and liked, doubling the ingredients as she went. As she wrote, she found herself stifling a few yawns. She looked up at the time to realize that it was nearly suppertime for the rest of the world, which meant it was past her bedtime. She had six hours to sleep before she started a full night of work, followed by a half day at the university, which, thankfully, she was fully prepared for.

Sarah rose and walked to the sink about to start washing the few dishes, but she stopped. Matt had offered to help. She didn't want to offend him by turning him down. Besides, with two people, the job would go twice as fast, and she could get to bed that much sooner.

She walked into the living room to ask him if he wanted to wash or dry. Instead of finding Matt sitting on the couch where she had left him, he was half-sitting, half-lying down. He had positioned himself with his long legs stretched out, one on the couch, the other dangling off. One arm lay draped across his stomach, the remote cradled in his large hand, the other hung limply at his side. His head was at what looked like a very awkward angle, tilted to one side, half on his shoulder and half resting against the back of the couch.

And he was snoring.

ten

An unknown presence brushed up against his chest.

Instinctively, Matt sprang to his feet. In a split second, he reached for his gun with his right hand, and thrust his left arm up to shield his body and block the perpetrator. He tensed and positioned himself with his feet planted firmly, ready to defend himself, by force if necessary.

As the world came into focus, he heard the sound of phasers blasting in the distance. Sarah stood in front of him, her eyes wide, her arms splayed at her sides as she pressed her back flat against the wall.

Matt let his body relax and dragged his hand over his face. "Oh, Sarah. . .I'm so sorry. I guess I dozed off."

"It's okay," she squeaked.

One look at her told him it wasn't okay.

He'd scared her. She still hadn't unpeeled herself from the wall.

Her voice lowered in pitch, but not by much. "I think it's time for you to go home."

Matt's heart sank. He couldn't remember ever having a day with such a high and such a low. He was supposed to be a pillar of strength, someone people could look up to. Yet, he'd let a situation get to him, and he'd completely lost it. Those people who died this morning were strangers. He'd been trained to handle horrific circumstances and stay calm and efficient when disaster threatened to overwhelm him. Yet, he'd done something he hadn't done since he was a little kid—he'd cried. Like a baby. Over people he didn't know.

When he was feeling like the world was sinking around him, Sarah hadn't judged him, she hadn't ridiculed him, and she hadn't made him feel foolish. She'd simply held him and let him work it out of his system. Her gentle touch and support helped lift the heavy weight off his shoulders.

She hadn't stopped there, either. Before long, she'd had him laughing out loud. He couldn't believe how much fun they had, just being silly. They'd even had somewhat of a pillow fight in her living room, using the small, decorative cushions off her couch to do battle. At first, he couldn't believe it when a pillow flew across the room and hit him in the head. Her little giggle was all it took for him to throw it right back—gently, of course. He'd never had a pillow fight in his life. He couldn't remember the last time he'd laughed like that, which told him it had been too long since he had fun.

When he first arrived, he couldn't help but notice how clean her apartment was, compared to the last time he was here. Maybe she'd gone through a little extra effort to tidy up, just for him. Although, judging by the state her apartment had been in a few days ago, it would have taken much longer than twenty-two minutes to clean. Yet, except for some smudges on the glass patio-door leading to the balcony, the place was clean. Not spotless, but comfortable.

While he was in the kitchen, he couldn't help but notice her calendar. She had the exact same days circled in different colors as he did on his own calendar at home.

She'd marked his schedule on her calendar.

He thought maybe, he just might be falling in love.

Sarah stepped away from the wall and smoothed out her sleeves, brushing off some imaginary dirt, no doubt needing more time to compose herself after he'd frightened her so badly.

He flexed his fingers and rammed his hands in his pockets, waiting for her to say more.

Earlier today, he'd thought she might have been feeling a little of the same thing he was, except now, she had just asked him to leave.

Maybe it wasn't such a bad thing that she didn't feel the same way. Both personally and professionally, seeing Sarah was a bad idea. First and foremost, the woman was a nonbeliever. Though she was sweet, kind, intelligent, and fun to be with, she didn't share his faith.

If he had been in any condition to be out that morning, he would have invited her to come to church again since she'd already been twice. Yet, he feared he was already in over his head, exactly where he didn't want to be. Already, he didn't trust himself to judge if she really did believe or if she was simply going along with him for reasons of her own.

As well, on a professional level, it was very bad to see each other socially. Without evidence, Sarah was the only witness they had who had seen money being exchanged between Kincaid and Donnie. She was also the only person who could identify Kincaid as an associate of Donnie. She saw when the contacts were made and how the money was passed on. She was the only one who could keep them under surveillance, and they not suspect they were being watched.

He continued to watch Sarah compose herself.

She looked so sweet and innocent that no one could ever suspect she was an informant. She was perfect.

She looked up at him, straight into his eyes. He couldn't look away. The deep, sea green drew him like a moth to a flame. "I don't want to be rude, but I really have to go to bed, so I think it's best that you go home. I think you could use some sleep, too, so that's also the best place for you."

Matt tried not to heave a sigh of relief. If her only reason for kicking him out was so that she could get some sleep before she went to work, then he could easily live with that.

He followed her to the door, but before she opened it, he blocked it with his foot and moved close to her. When she didn't shy away, he slowly raised his hand until he brushed her cheek with his fingertips. He had so much to say, and so much was rolling around in his mind, he didn't know where to start.

He cleared his throat, but he still could hardly speak. "Thanks for dinner."

Very slowly, she raised her hand until she loosely wrapped her fingers around his wrist. Her voice came out lower in pitch than usual, almost husky. "You're welcome."

The silky sound made his heart race and her touch made his brain misfire. He reached up with his other hand until he cradled her cheeks in both hands. She still didn't move away, nor did she show any signs of hesitation.

"Sarah. . . ," he muttered as he lowered his head to hers, letting his voice trail off when his lips touched hers. Slowly and gently, he kissed her warm, soft lips. She lifted her head just a little within the cradle of his hands and returned his kiss.

Matt's heart kicked into overdrive. He wanted to slip his arms around her back and hold her tight and kiss her well and good, but this wasn't the right time for that. Using all the self-control he could muster, he pulled back and let his arms fall to his sides. "Bye, Sarah. I guess I'll see you around."

Before she could tell him that wasn't such a good idea, he turned, opened the door, and left.

٭

With a shaking hand, Sarah hung up the phone. All night long at the donut shop and all through classes, she'd been unable to concentrate. No matter what she tried to do, and no matter what she did, all her thoughts drifted back to Matt. That she'd gotten his answering machine instead of talking to him in person was probably a blessing in disguise. She probably couldn't have put together an intelligent sentence right now if she had to speak to him in person.

He'd kissed her.

Fool that she was, she'd kissed him back.

Sarah squeezed her eyes shut. She didn't know what she was doing with Matt. All she knew was that it wasn't smart.

She couldn't allow herself to get emotionally involved with a cop. His normal days weren't as exciting and intriguing as what she saw on television, but danger was a reality on his job. He wasn't James Bond, and he didn't face life-threatening situations every day, but he still did face them. All it took was once for something to go wrong. Even if he didn't die on the job, divorce rates among cops were high. The stress level of his job was high. People couldn't help but let their job overflow as part of their personalities into their off-duty lives. That kind of stress took its toll not only on a person, but also on their spouse.

Matt was every inch a cop, and he didn't have to be in uniform. Just looking at him she could tell, even if she'd never met him before.

Until yesterday, she told herself the reason he was seeing her when he wasn't on duty was because she'd first gone to seek him out, to tell him something that related to his being on duty.

She had obviously only been fooling herself. The way he kissed her had nothing to do with duty.

Unless. . .it was a delayed reaction after the trauma of being with the little boy who died.

With her hand still pressed on the phone, Sarah stared blankly at the table. The recipes she'd written out for Matt, and then forgotten to give him after his rather abrupt awakening, were still there.

She still wanted to give them to him. Regardless of how she felt about the possibility of developing a relationship with him, as he said, the man still had to eat. Even if she didn't want to go further, he was a nice guy. And he was an awfully good kisser.

Sarah buried her face in her hands. She couldn't allow herself to think like that. From this day forward, it would be business only with Matt. Because of the situation at the donut shop, she would still see Matt, the cop. But she would no longer see Matt, the man.

❧

Today's line of customers somehow seemed to be worse than usual. Still, Sarah found working the counter preferable to the drive-thru for the morning rush. This way, she didn't have to put up with the exhaust fumes drifting in her face or get a blast of cold morning air every time she opened the window. Tomorrow, she would have the drive-thru, and Kristie would get the counter.

She pushed in the cash drawer, anxious to serve the next customer as soon as the group of four ladies moved out of the way. As they lifted their individual cups and started to clear some space for the next customer, a tall man in a dark suit stepped up to the counter.

Sarah's breath caught. "Matt?" She glanced from side to side and cleared her throat. "I mean Constable Walker. How nice to see you today."

He grinned like the cat that swallowed the canary. "Hi, Sarah." His smooth voice almost made her knees buckle. "I'll have a Boston Cream and a large vanilla latté."

She looked up at him, then to the entrance to the washrooms. No other officer appeared to be in the building. She couldn't see the parking lot through the crowd, so she couldn't tell if his were the only police cruiser in the lot.

Today, Matt was still wearing his hat inside the building, which he never did when he came in at night for his coffee breaks. Not only was he in uniform, he was in full uniform, including a tie and the jacket, smartly buttoned.

She lowered her voice. "What are you doing here all by yourself? At this hour? It's seven-thirty in the morning."

He smiled as he reached into his pocket, pulled out his wallet, and handed her some money. "I'm a cop. This is a donut shop. There's nowhere else I'd rather be."

Someone behind him giggled.

Sarah rang his order into the cash register and counted back his change. "Right."

"I'm on my way to a court hearing so I thought I'd pick up a donut and a coffee. Since I won't be called out, I can actually drink it before it gets cold."

"Oh. I guess that means you want this to go." She turned and hit the button on the latté machine while she put the donut in a bag for him.

"How're things? Same as usual?"

Sarah glanced quickly around him, at the crowd of people

both in her line, as well as in Casey's. Kristie's line at the drive-thru had to be twenty cars long. Sarah didn't know if he just meant in general, or if his question was in some kind of secret code, and she was supposed to tell him if Kincaid had been back with another suitcase for Donnie, which he hadn't. She didn't know how to word a coded reply. "Everything's been about the same as usual, I guess."

He nodded as she slid the coffee across the counter. "Good. Bye, Sarah."

Matt walked out of the donut shop, holding himself straight and tall and ever so handsome.

Not only she, but a number of people in the lines also watched him, especially the women.

Sarah gritted her teeth. She didn't want to care that the other women watched him. She had no claim on him, nor did she ever intend to have a claim on him.

Before she could think about why it bothered her, Sarah leaned forward to the woman who was first in her lineup. "Excuse me, Ma'am? What would you like?"

The woman, her cheeks a brilliant shade of red, turned back to Sarah and mumbled her order.

For the last portion of her morning, Sarah scrambled to shorten her line. By the time the woman who replaced her arrived, Sarah was tired, and she'd had enough.

On her way through the kitchen, as she headed for the staff room to change, she nearly lost her footing on a pile of sprinkles that had been spilled on the floor.

She sighed and turned toward the closet to get the broom. She didn't have a lot of time to spare before her first class of the morning, but she would feel too guilty if someone else slipped on the same pile and was hurt.

When she opened the closet door, she didn't immediately turn on the light. With the light out, she looked down to see the glow of the light from Donnie's office, reflecting through.

Sarah stepped backward, turned around, and scanned the

room. Everyone else was busy with customers, and the kitchen was vacant.

Tamping down her curiosity had never been easy for Sarah. She couldn't help herself. Since no one was watching, she slipped into the closet without turning on the light and quietly pushed the door closed behind her. Dropping to her knees, she inched along the floor and looked up through the vent.

Donnie was alone in his office, sitting behind his desk. The increasingly familiar briefcase lay open beside him. This time, Sarah hadn't seen Kincaid come in, but that didn't necessarily mean he hadn't. The same as every day, when the morning rush began, she concentrated on each customer who was in front of her, not on who was coming in the door or where they went. She knew that the suitcase had only recently been delivered. Otherwise, it would already be in the safe.

Knowing that Kincaid had been in and she missed him, Sarah told herself that from now on, she would pay more attention to the door, regardless of the crowd. The fact that he was no longer limiting his visits to the middle of the night, when everything was quiet, sent shivers down her spine.

Sarah gritted her teeth and inched closer to the vent, trying to catch a glimpse of the contents of the briefcase. If there was again money in it, she had to tell Matt. However, from her angle next to the floor and looking up, she couldn't determine the contents.

She could determine, though, that in addition to the usual briefcase, a black duffel bag was also lying on top of the desk.

Sarah held her breath as Donnie put down the bundle of money he had been counting. He reached into the duffel bag and pulled something out. A sly smile grew on his face as he examined the contents of his hand. He started to poke at whatever was in his palm, but the phone rang. At the sound, a small sandwich bag filled with white powder dropped out of his hand and onto the desk. Some of the contents of the bag must have spilled, because Donnie muttered a string of very crude words. He cleared his throat and answered the phone as politely as he usually did while he brushed the powder from the surface of the desk and back into the bag.

Something in Sarah's stomach churned, and she knew it wasn't because she was hungry. She didn't know exactly what Donnie had, but unless she was mistaken, it was something very illegal.

She didn't need to see more. While Donnie was still talking, Sarah shuffled backward, stood, and grabbed the broom and dustpan. Without turning on the light, she slowly opened the door and peeked out. No one had come into the kitchen yet, so she quickly slipped out and did the quickest sweep job she'd ever done in her life. Without changing into her regular clothes, she hustled out of the building, into her car, and drove straight to the police station.

eleven

"16Bravo4. Back in service."

"16Bravo4. While you were in court, that same woman who was in here last week left another message asking you to call her. Do you need the number?"

Matt's stomach tightened. The only other time Sarah had left a message at the station was when she could make a positive identification on Kincaid exchanging money with Donnie. He had no doubt that for her to, once more, run into the station on her way to the university meant something equally as important had happened. "I have it." He checked the time. "I've got to add this to my calls today. It's a follow-up to a current file. Was there any specific message?"

"No message, just the phone number."

Matt gave the dispatcher Sarah's address and checked the time. He had to trust that if it were something urgent, she would have said so.

Matt took care of two of the prior calls that had backed up while he was in court in order to time himself to arrive at her apartment building shortly after she arrived home from classes.

He drove onto Sarah's street at the same time as he saw her little blue car disappear into the entrance for the underground parking.

He punched a *ten-seven* into the computer to let dispatch know that he was out of service unless something urgent came up and quickly entered a few notes about his last call. Once he figured he'd given Sarah enough time to park her car and get up to her apartment, he locked up the squad car and made his way to the main entrance of the apartment building.

This time, she answered his buzz only a few seconds after he pressed the button. She wasn't waiting for him at the elevator, but when he arrived at her door, it opened before he knocked.

"I just got home a couple of minutes ago. Your timing is great. Would you like me to make coffee?"

Matt glanced over Sarah's shoulder into her apartment. In order to talk at a location away from the scene of the alleged crime, they had no alternative but to meet on personal territory—his church, her home, or in a public restaurant—when he was on his personal time. But this time, he was in uniform and on duty. For reasons of personal safety, it was against department policy for an officer in uniform to accept food or drink from anyone, including trusted informants. He knew Sarah was safe, but still, if he let her make him coffee, the visit would feel too social, and for him, at that moment, it was very much business.

Up until now, because he liked Sarah, he'd conveniently forgotten why they had come together in the first place. He was an upholder of the law. He was there to investigate a crime in progress. She was finished working, and in the comfort of her own home, but he wasn't.

Therefore, Matt remained standing in the foyer, just as he would have if he were questioning someone he didn't know.

"I'd better pass on the coffee. But thanks for asking. What happened?"

"I didn't see Kincaid today. He must have been there when the place was busy. Donnie had more money. The more money I see, the more I'm pretty sure they're laundering money. How is it done?"

"Commonly it's filtered through legitimate businesses in phony sales and supplier invoices, and there would be many bank accounts set up in different names under false identifications. Everything has to run through consistently and not in sporadic huge lump sums so it doesn't cause any raised eyebrows at the taxation department. Most is done through independent, non-franchised businesses."

"Just like Donnie's Donuts. So that means this could have been going on for a long time. Years even."

"Yes, that's what it means. Although, in this case, I tend to doubt it's been that long." Matt happened to know that Kincaid had only been out of jail for seven months. "Didn't you tell me that Donnie has only been coming in for the graveyard shift for the last six months or so? Tell me, didn't you think it was a bit unusual for the owner to be coming in and working in the middle of the night?"

Sarah shook he head. "No. Donnie had just fired a really awful night manager, and that's when he started coming in late. I thought he was having a hard time finding a reliable manager, and he'd eventually hire someone. Kristie and I got used to seeing him, and it's normal now. But I'm working graveyard shift because I'm going to school during the daytime. Maybe Donnie has something else to do during the daytime too."

Matt didn't want to think of what Donnie could have been doing during the daytime if he was taking in Kincaid's drug money at night.

Since turning in his original report to the shift NCO, he'd discussed his findings with the staff sergeant and had been assigned as the officer in charge. The department had gone over what was happening at Donnie's Donuts at a couple of recent debriefings. Apparently, Kincaid was already under suspicion. After being seen repeatedly at Donnie's, a general bulletin had been put out for all members to keep an eye on things.

Being a donut shop, open twenty-four/seven, it was an easy thing to do. Since his report had been officially discussed, more and more members of the force were gradually filtering through Donnie's on their breaks at varying times of the day and night, hoping to see something. The staff sergeant had instructed all the members to take their breaks at Donnie's and treat it as a callout, just to keep a constant eye on things. Already some of them had noticed suspicious activity going out the back door.

Not wanting to give Kincaid or Donnie any indication that the police knew something was going on, the timing of their surveillance had to be increased very gradually. Their biggest downfall was that a member in uniform, even on breaks, wasn't a very subtle form of observation. They hadn't been able to gather enough evidence of a magnitude that would justify an undercover surveillance team. The last thing they could afford to do was have Kincaid and Donnie shut down or move the operation because the place was suddenly swarming with cops.

So far, their best source of information was from someone working on the inside, and that someone was Sarah. With what appeared to be "only" money laundering happening, at least as far as Donnie was concerned, Matt figured that if she were careful not to be noticed, and if she were careful that no one saw her talking to the police, she was safe. The RCMP would eventually get their man.

Matt removed his notepad from his pocket and scribbled down some notes. "So you saw more money, but you didn't see how it came in."

"Wait. That's not all. Today I saw something else."

Matt's hand froze midword. With Kincaid involved, a sensation of dread coursed through him.

"I saw Donnie with drugs today. And it wasn't medicine-type drugs. It was the bad kind."

"What exactly was it? Do you know how much there was?"

She shook her head and crossed her arms over her chest. "I couldn't see that well through the vent, and remember, the vent is right next to the floor, so I was looking up. I only know that it was a black duffel bag, about twice the size of my purse. I saw it on the desk when Donnie was counting the money. When he finished with the money, he reached into the black bag and pulled out a sandwich bag full of white powder. He dropped the bag on the desk when the phone rang, and some powder spilled out. That's how I saw it."

Matt stiffened from head to foot. What they were talking about was probably either heroine or cocaine. As accurately as he could recall, Sarah's purse wasn't huge. However, it was large enough for her to hold a book, her umbrella, plus the regular paraphernalia women liked to carry around for no good reason.

In that case, if the only contents of the duffel bag in question were drugs, then the quantity was far more than could be considered reasonable for personal use.

This was trafficking. Kincaid was supplying. Donnie was selling to pushers.

Sarah was right in the middle of it.

The concept that she wouldn't be in danger dissolved like a sugar cube in a cup of hot coffee. Suddenly, everything had become very complicated. Not only was Donnie laundering Kincaid's money, he was also selling some of Kincaid's drugs. They still had to follow Kincaid around and see where he was getting them. The department would be happy they'd pinpointed where some of Kincaid's supply was going. Now they would have to determine to whom Donnie was selling it and at what level.

"What do you think Donnie's doing with all that stuff?"

"I don't know. We'll have to find out. Somehow."

Her eyebrows arched. She snapped her heels together and lifted one hand in the form of a salute. "Detective Cunningham, on duty, Sir!"

Matt sucked in a deep breath. When he'd called her *Detective*, he had only been joking around. There was nothing funny about what she was implying she would do. Quite the opposite, the situation was spiraling out of control and becoming more dangerous every time she came to him with additional information.

"This isn't television, Sarah. It's not as easy as it initially looks. There are real risks involved. This is no child's game."

"I know that. I don't know how to describe what it was like to watch Donnie and then get out of there before anyone saw me and then tell you about it. It's kinda fun and kinda scary at the same time. Know what I mean?"

She smiled from ear to ear, but Matt didn't feel much like smiling back. He knew exactly what she meant.

As a police officer, he was well aware of the adrenaline rush when working a dangerous case. But he was a professional, fully trained, with a few years of experience under his belt.

And when worse came to worst, he was big and he had a

twelve

"Matt, can I talk to you for a minute?"

"Yeah, just a sec," Matt muttered as he finished the last sentence of the last report for the day. He looked up to see the staff sergeant standing beside the workstation. "What's up, Jeff?"

"I read your last report on what's happening at Donnie's Donuts. Can I ask you something about where you got your information?"

Matt's heart nearly stopped. He breathed deeply and forced himself to grin as he leaned back in the chair with his body at an angle, stretched out one leg, and slung one arm over the back of the chair. "What do you need to know?"

"Your informant. How did you get her?"

Matt forced himself to breath evenly. "She came to me, actually."

"What's she like? How well do you know her?"

Matt's heart picked up its pace. He didn't want to talk about how well he knew Sarah. "I don't know how to answer that. Why do you ask?"

"I see you noted that she wants to remain anonymous when we do the bust. I'm sure we can do that. I was wondering if she could maybe help us speed things up and save the department a few dollars. Do you think she'd be willing to give us a call next time Kincaid walks in, so we can get someone down there right away to follow him and see where he goes? It would help us see where this latest batch is coming from."

"She doesn't have a cell phone. I'm not sure that's a good idea, anyway. I don't want anyone seeing her placing calls like that from the premises. If Kincaid found out he was being followed after seeing Sarah make a quick phone call, that would put her at considerable risk."

Matt realized he made a mistake by referring to Sarah by her first name when Jeff's eyebrows rose. "Point taken. Are you emotionally involved with your informant?"

Matt stared up at Jeff. He knew the department's policy on a member keeping an emotional distance from a witness, which was what Sarah might later turn out to be should the situation go to court. They always tried to keep informants away from court, but occasionally they did have to use them as witnesses when the case went to trial. If it did in this case, once again Kincaid would have a high-priced and unscrupulous lawyer. Unless they actually caught Kincaid red-handed, which Matt doubted they would, any and all evidence would rest with the only witness, which in this case would be Sarah.

First, the defense would do everything they could to discredit the witness. Kincaid's lawyer would establish that a relationship existed between the witness and the officer in charge, which was himself. They would then slant the questions and badger the witness to "prove" that the police officer in charge had coached the witness, guiding her in her testimony and actions, to the detriment of the accused. After drawing the only evidence they had into question, the judge would have no alternative but to throw the case out of court. Matt didn't want that to happen. Not this time.

Sarah had been right when she said his desire to put Kincaid behind bars was personal. But above all else, he wanted Sarah to be safe. Now that there were drugs involved, staying safe would be harder to do.

At this point, he didn't know from one minute to the next how emotionally involved he was with Sarah. Nor did it matter. She wasn't a Christian, so he wasn't about to marry her. The point was he loved her enough to keep his own needs separate. No matter what happened, no matter how she felt about him, he had to keep her safe.

He'd told her to keep out of the closet and stop spying on Donnie, but in his gut, he knew she wouldn't. The only way to keep her safe would be to keep tabs on her himself. He couldn't do that if they pulled him from the case and put someone else as the officer in charge.

"The issue here is keeping a civilian safe. She's an innocent and only doing what she feels is the right thing to do. I wouldn't care if the informant were male or female. It's not a good idea to have them making calls like that from their place of employment when it can't be done in private."

"I had to ask. Does your informant think anyone else there is involved or just the owner?"

"We haven't talked about it. So far it's just the owner." Nor did he want Sarah poking around. However, Jeff's question further reminded Matt that Sarah's last comment had been about watching for other suspicious characters. He hadn't broached the subject of the other employees, nor had he had time to respond properly. The thought opened up a whole new area of risk.

"Okay. Just wondering. See you next time you're on dayshift, Matt."

Matt stood. "Yeah. See you, Jeff." He quickly turned and walked to the locker room to stow his equipment and change.

Tomorrow was another day. The day he was going to get Sarah to behave herself and stay safe.

❧

Sarah sighed and looked around her apartment. For the first time in weeks, the whole place was clean, except for the unmade bed and a bit of laundry piled in the corner, which didn't really count. Because she'd finally managed to catch up and get ahead on her homework and assigned reading, she finally caught up on her housework.

For today, she could read for pleasure. She picked up a book Gwen had loaned her months ago, a Heartsong Presents novel by Gwen's favorite author. She settled back on the couch and began to read, but she barely made it past the first page when the buzzer for the main door sounded.

When she hit the button, a deep, flowing male voice came over the speaker. "Hi Sarah. It's lunchtime. I brought food."

"Matt?" Sarah looked around the apartment one more time, just in case she missed something on her earlier cleaning spree. "Uh, come on up."

Since she only had to close the bedroom door, Sarah stepped into the hall to wait for Matt as he came up the elevator. When the door opened, the fragrance of pizza radiating from the largest pizza box she had ever seen reached her before Matt did. Balanced on top of the pizza box, were two large cups of flavored coffee.

"What are you doing here? What if I wasn't home?"

He grinned. Something funny happened in her stomach, making her realize she must have been hungry after all. "Then I'd eat this whole pizza myself."

"I guess." She turned around and led Matt into the kitchen.

She took the plates and napkins out of the cupboard while Matt centered the pizza box on the table and placed a coffee at each setting.

"I'm really surprised to see you today. I thought you usually went to the gym on your stretch between dayshift and nightshift."

"I wanted to see you instead. Do you like anchovies and olives?"

Her stomach churned. "Ugh, no!"

"Good. Me neither. I brought ham and pineapple." He flipped the box open.

She couldn't help but smile at him. "How did that call go?"

"What call?" he mumbled as he carefully lifted two slices of pizza to each plate.

"That one that made you run out of here so fast yesterday."

His eyebrows quirked, then he grinned. "Oh, that. It went well. Great, actually."

He sat in one of the chairs and folded his hands on the table. This time, Sarah knew what to expect, so she also folded her hands on the table and bowed her head.

"Dear Lord, thank You for this food before us and for friends to share it with. I ask for Your blessings on this day and for every day to come. Amen."

"Amen."

He took a big bite. "Good, isn't it?" he asked through his mouthful.

Sarah only nodded as she ate, not wanting to be rude.

"When I got to the warehouse, I was alone for a few minutes. No one likes to check out robberies in progress in industrial areas all alone, but the other member wasn't due for five minutes, and I heard movement inside the building. I know five minutes doesn't sound like a long time, but it is when there was only one of me, and I could hear three or four voices inside the building. We never know if it's just kids checking things out, getting a thrill out of being where they shouldn't be, or if there are really thieves who know what they're after and are prepared for the risk they're taking of being caught. We also don't know if they're armed, and if they are armed, if they're experienced with a gun."

Sarah pressed her palms to her cheeks. "What did you do?"

"I knew they'd never listen to me if they knew I was alone, so I told them I was going to send the dog in."

"I didn't know you had a dog."

He grinned. "I don't have a dog. I'm not a K-9 unit. But they didn't know that. I barked a couple of times, told myself, 'down boy,' and then said if they didn't come out, one at a time with their hands up, the dog was going in. I also called out to the other member that I'd located them. They didn't know he wasn't there yet. It was a bunch of kids, and they came out. They never did know I didn't really have a dog; they thought the dog was back in the car. I had two of them cuffed by the time Rick got there."

He stopped to laugh and wiped his mouth with his napkin. "You do what you gotta do. Sometimes the good guys really do win."

All Sarah could do was stare at Matt as he continued to snicker to himself.

She didn't think he was very funny. The only thing she could think of was how potentially dangerous the situation could have been. Yet, he was unbothered, like it was a normal, every-day occurrence. Maybe for him it was. She had to admire his ingenuity. No one was hurt, and even though he was so badly outnumbered, he single-handedly caught the criminals. But she also knew he'd taken a big risk. If they had looked outside and seen him all alone barking like a dog, the outcome could have been very different.

The concept scared her witless.

Matt took a sip of his coffee and lowered the cup to the table. "While I'm here, I was wondering if we could talk about what's going on at Donnie's."

"I thought we talked about this yesterday."

He helped himself to another large slice of pizza. "Not really. Besides, last night I was talking about the case to the staff sergeant. He asked a few questions about my informant. That's you."

Sarah nearly forgot to breathe. "Informant?" she squeaked. Visions of filthy and desperate junkies with long, unwashed hair making clandestine meetings with undercover cops all dressed in black flashed through her mind. She was none of the above.

"Jeff, he's one of the staff sergeants, mentioned about coworkers. He reminded me that we haven't talked about everyone else who works there. If other employees might be involved or have seen something, it's not a good idea to poke around and ask questions. Yes, we want to know, but if you start asking people, your cover is blown. And with the likes of Kincaid, that would be very dangerous."

"Then what am I supposed to do?"

As soon as the words left her mouth, she realized what she had done. She had just admitted, in not so many words, that figuratively she was going to stay out of the closet, but she hadn't intended to stop looking for information that would lead to Kincaid's arrest, even if that meant Donnie would go down with him. Not only was the money laundering illegal, the source that money was coming from was drugs, and now Donnie was selling drugs too. She couldn't *not* do something when she had an opportunity to stop an ongoing problem to society. She thought of all the children she would be teaching when she finally finished at the university and how badly children and teens could get messed up on drugs. She would do whatever could be done to get the pushers off the streets.

"All you can do is watch and listen. If you hear other staff talking and something comes up that sounds suspicious, tell me about it. Then the police can decide if it means anything. I guess what I'm trying to say is, all I want you to do is keep your eyes and ears open and don't do anything else."

"And stay out of the closet."

"That's especially where I don't want you to go." Matt lifted a piece of pizza to his face and opened his mouth.

"But what if I need the broom?"

Matt froze. He sighed, closed his mouth, and lowered the pizza to his plate. "You know what I mean. By the way, while I was out today, I bought you something." He leaned to one side and patted a cell phone on the side of his belt. "And I bought this for me."

While he was still sitting crooked, Matt pulled a small velvet bag out of his pocket.

Sarah's breath caught. The bag he held was specifically for jewelry. As he untied the silk string, she saw the outline of something round at the bottom of the bag. The only round piece of jewelry she could think of was a ring.

She didn't want a ring from Matt. A ring meant emotional connection. Commitment. It implied a relationship. She didn't want to get involved in a relationship that had no possibility of a future. She couldn't contemplate a life of being married to a man who one day might never come home from work. Therefore, she wasn't going to let such a relationship begin.

It didn't matter what kind of ring it was. Even if it were a simple mood ring. She couldn't accept it.

Before she could think of a way to turn him down that wouldn't hurt his feelings, he poked two fingers in the bag, and groped inside. Slowly, he started to pull his fingers out. Along with his fingers followed a gold chain.

Sarah allowed herself to breathe. As he repositioned his grasp on the bag, she recognized the logo as that of a well-known, fine-quality jewelry store. The logo and the bright shine of the chain told her it was real gold. A chain, she could accept, although she felt hesitant about accepting something so expensive.

She didn't know why Matt would want to buy her something so fine, especially jewelry. He'd kissed her once, but that had been under emotional duress. They didn't have the kind of relationship that warranted expensive jewelry. Still, she couldn't *not* accept it. Even though Matt, the cop, frightened her, she was becoming increasingly fond of Matt, the man. Out of uniform, she liked him very much.

As the last part of the chain appeared from the bag, so did a round pendant about the size of a penny, dangling from the chain. It appeared to be a locket, because it had a small clasp on one side. However, the gold color of the pendant didn't shine the same way as the necklace. On the locket's case was a strange embossed pattern more suited for a child than an adult. Considering the cost and beauty of the necklace, the size and quality of the locket didn't match.

He slid his chair closer to hers. "Turn around, and I'll put it on you."

She didn't turn around immediately. Instead, she watched Matt, with his large fingers, fumbling with the dainty clasp. Sarah knew she could open it easier than he could, but she didn't want to spoil the moment for him.

When he finally managed to open it, he held the necklace open. Sarah squirmed in the chair so her back was mostly toward him so he could drape the chain around her neck and refasten the clasp.

"I want you to wear this, especially when you're at work."

She raised one hand and pressed the locket to her chest. The chain itself was virtually weightless, but in comparison, the locket felt quite heavy. She found it very odd that Matt would choose such a fine chain, and, to put it bluntly, pick such an ugly, mismatched locket.

"Thank you. This is such a surprise. Is there a picture of you inside?"

She ran her fingers along the grain of the pattern. She didn't want to like Matt, but she couldn't help herself, she did. She hoped against hope that he had put a picture of himself inside.

"Nope. No picture. It's a transmitter."

Sarah's fingers froze in the center of the locket. "It's a what?"

"Open it. Can you feel the little button in there? That was the only locket I could find that would fit the housing. I glued it inside."

As instructed, she flipped the clasp. She craned her neck and tried to focus on what should have been a picture. Sure enough, a small metal casing with a red button in the middle was glued inside the locket.

"How romantic. . . ," she muttered.

Once more, he patted the cell phone, then reached for another piece of pizza. "If you push that button, I've got the receiver here. It's set to vibrate and not ring so I can wear it when I'm on duty. If I can't attend, I'll radio for backup, and someone else will come. Just remember, with no ability for voice transmission, you have to understand that if you push it, I'll assume you're at Donnie's Donuts, and that's where I'll go. The vibration-only kind was the only one that would fit inside a small locket. The ones that can transmit a voice are too big to hide."

Visions of the commercial for infirmed or elderly people living on their own, wearing similar things around their necks, flashed through her mind. She reached up and ran her fingers through her still-brown hair.

"I don't know what to say."

Matt wiped his mouth with the napkin and dropped it on the plate. He'd eaten at least half a large pizza by himself, just for lunch. "Say you'll wear it every second you're at Donnie's Donuts, and if something happens, you'll push the button."

She snapped the locket closed. "I will."

Matt stood. "Great. Before I go back to bed, I've got a few things to do to get ready for work tonight, so I've got to go. You can finish the rest of the pizza."

Sarah stood as well, and followed him to the door. Just as the last time when she saw him out, as she reached for the doorknob, one of his feet blocked the way, so she couldn't open the door.

He reached down and gently lifted the locket and ran his thumb over it. "I'm worried about you, Sarah. This has mushroomed into much more than simple money laundering. If Kincaid is supplying drugs to Donnie, he's supplying elsewhere. With his history, this could be the catalyst to a very big drug operation."

Still touching the locket, Matt used his other hand to tip up her chin. "Stay safe, Sarah," he muttered. His head lowered, and his eyes began to flutter shut. "Please stay safe. For me."

She couldn't help it. Before their lips met, Sarah had already closed her eyes. When his mouth covered hers, Sarah thought her knees would buckle. He kissed her so sweetly she had to hold onto his waist for dear life.

Too soon, he pulled away. "See you around sometime," he mumbled as he opened the door and left.

Sarah stood with her feet frozen to the floor, staring at the back of the closed apartment door.

Once again, she touched the locket and ran her fingers over the pattern. Her eyes started to burn, and she blinked to keep them from overflowing. Coming from Matt, the locket, such as it was, truly was the most romantic gift she'd ever received. Even though it was only meant to wear to work, she wondered if maybe she'd never take it off.

She turned around and walked into the bathroom to look at herself in the mirror, wearing the locket.

The transmitter really was totally concealed and inconspicuous. Just like something out of a James Bond movie.

And that gave Sarah an idea.

thirteen

Sarah started the car, but she couldn't drive away. Not yet.

The pastor's words echoed through her head, and she couldn't turn them off.

She picked up the bulletin, which she'd scribbled full of notes as the pastor talked, and she read what she'd written.

She wanted to talk to Matt, but he had gotten off work at seven o'clock that morning, if he got off on time. He was going back to work at seven that night, and he needed his sleep. Her next choice would have been Gwen, except she knew Gwen and Lionel were going to Gwen's mother's house for lunch.

Therefore, Sarah did the only other thing she could think of. She turned off the car and stomped back into the church. Going against the flow of the people, she made her way all the way to the front, where the pastor was standing talking to someone. When the other person moved away, Sarah stepped forward.

"Excuse me, Pastor? Can I ask you something?"

He smiled. "Certainly."

"You said this morning that doing good deeds won't get you into heaven, but you can't get into heaven without doing good deeds. I don't get it."

The pastor wrinkled his brow while he thought for a minute. "Good question. Think of it this way. Do you believe in Jesus Christ as your Lord and Savior?"

"I. . ." Sarah let her voice trail off. She'd listened to the pastor talk about believing in Jesus for four weeks in a row. She thought back to the things she'd been taught as a child, when her neighbor used to take her and any of the other neighborhood kids who would go to church. She thought of the things Matt had said about Jesus and how Jesus died so that those who believed would have eternal life. This morning, the pastor had read the very same thing right out of the Bible, which was God's Word.

She believed in God, and she believed that what God said in the Bible was true.

"Yes. I think I do," she said.

The pastor crossed his arms and smiled. "If you're not sure, then think of it this way. If you left for work, and halfway there you thought you left an element on when you were cooking. Would you turn around and be late for work to go home and turn it off?"

"Well, no. I probably would have thought I was imagining it and hadn't left it on, so no, I wouldn't go back."

"Then you didn't really believe you left it on. If you really believed, you would go back, even if it made you late, and your boss docked your pay. It's the same way when you believe in Jesus as your Lord and Savior. Even bad people do some good deeds, for their own reasons. Are you doing good deeds just because it feels good to do them, or because Jesus wants you to, even if they are hard to do or cost you something? If you do something only because Jesus wants you to, then you really believe."

Sarah's head swam. Matt hadn't explained it like that.

"That's the difference. If you believe in Jesus and love Him, then you will do the good deeds because He wants you to, regardless of the cost. It's the motivation that makes the difference to God. He also says that when you see something that needs to be done, if you love Jesus, you do it because He is Lord of your life. Talk is cheap. God wants action to prove your faith, because it's the faith that opens the doors to Heaven."

"The Bible says that?"

"Not in exactly those words, but, yes, it says that." He reached over to a nearby table, picked up a Bible, and paged through it. "Right here in the book of James. See where it is?"

A sinking feeling hit Sarah in the stomach. She did believe, but she'd never thought about having to prove it. Did she really believe enough to want to prove it? "I think I had better do some reading. Do you know where I can go to get a Bible?"

The pastor lost his smile. "I'd give you one, but the Sunday school gave the last one away today. You can get a Bible from the Christian book store a few blocks away."

Sarah checked her watch. "Great. I'll go there."

The pastor smiled again. "You'll have to wait until tomorrow. They're closed on Sundays."

Sarah nodded. "Okay. Then I'll make a stop on my way home from the university tomorrow. Thanks for your help. I should go now."

Sarah drove straight home. She found herself pacing. She really wanted to understand but didn't want to wait a full twenty-four hours before she could start reading. Not only did Matt own a Bible, but his was also filled with all sorts of nicely written notes that would probably help her understand.

She looked at the clock. If Matt had to be at the station for his debriefing at 6:30, he probably woke up at 5:45 or sooner. He would probably loan her his Bible for a day until she could buy her own. If she picked it up before he had to go to work, she could dash home and do a little reading before she had to lie down and have a nap to get herself charged and ready for work at midnight.

Sarah smiled at her own ingenuity. She quickly changed into her pajamas, and set the alarm for 6:00 P.M.

≈

"I'm gone for lunch break, Kristie. Can you watch the front for me?"

"Sure thing."

Sarah nearly ran to the lunchroom. The first thing she did was dig Matt's Bible out of her purse and open it up to where she had her bookmark. Once settled, she lifted her sandwich, about to take her first bite, and froze. Matt always prayed before he ate. If he were in public, he closed his eyes for just a second and prayed silently. But when in a private place, he took the time to do it properly.

Sarah laid her sandwich back down on the plate, folded her hands on the table, and closed her eyes.

Dear God. This is my first time doing this, so I hope I'm doing it right. Thanks for this food and thanks for this job and thanks for Matt, who really is a great guy. Amen.

Matt.

With her palm, she pressed the locket to her chest, over her heart. Matt had been utterly shocked when she phoned to ask if she could borrow his Bible. His expression had been priceless when he answered the door. She knew he'd be in a rush to leave for work, so she hadn't stayed. He'd barely had time to stammer that she could have his Bible as long as she wanted before she ran off with it and drove home.

As she ate her lunch, she read all the parts that the pastor had talked about, some of them two or three times, until she felt she understood them. Unfortunately, she didn't have time to read any more before her time was up, and she had to return to work.

Upon her return to switch off at the counter with Kristie, Kristie's gaze flitted to the locket.

Her eyes narrowed as she studied it, then examined the chain. "Did you find your old locket from when you were a kid? That retro look is really in right now, although I personally draw the line at bad jewelry. I guess that locket must be special. Have you got an old picture of your mom and dad in there?"

"It's not from my mom and dad. It's from a friend." The second the words left Sarah's mouth, she snapped her big mouth shut.

Kristie's eyes widened. "You mean it's new? I'm so sorry! I didn't mean to insult your locket, especially if it was a gift. What kind of friend? A boyfriend?"

"I. . ." Sarah let her voice trail off. She didn't want to say it was from Matt, because when he came into the donut shop, he was on duty. She couldn't tell Kristie not to say anything around Donnie that she was seeing a cop. If Donnie found out, he'd automatically become defensive, and she didn't want him to try harder to cover up what he was doing. She was actually hoping he'd get sloppy. Suddenly, an idea came to her. She forced herself to laugh, hoping it didn't sound fake. "Yes, it's from my new boyfriend, who obviously has questionable taste in jewelry. But I have to wear it, or I'd hurt his feelings."

"Is he cute?"

Matt's handsome smiling face with his beautiful blue eyes flashed through her mind. Sarah sighed. "Yes, he's cute."

Kristie reached out in the direction of the locket. "Then bad taste is okay. Can I see his picture?"

In a flash, Sarah covered the locket with her palm to protect it. "I have to get a good picture of him."

"Oh, he's shy, huh? That's okay. Just make sure and point him out to me if he ever comes in here."

"If I remember. I think it's time for your lunch break now."

Kristie had only been gone for fifteen minutes when Matt and another officer came in. She tried to tamp down her smile as they walked up the center aisle toward the counter.

"Good evening, gentlemen. What will it be tonight? I'll bet this is. . ." Sarah glanced at Matt. As she did so, she raised her hand and touched the locket. He lowered his eyes for a split second only to acknowledge her movement, then quickly resumed direct eye contact. ". . .a bran muffin and mocha cream night for you, Constable Walker. And for Constable Edwards, a cheese scone and a House-Blend Special."

Both officers smiled, Matt more than Constable Edwards. Imagining his smile earlier in no way compared to the real thing, which almost made her knees weak.

"Sounds good," they both replied. Sarah quickly prepared their orders and set everything on the counter. She rested her palms on the table and waited for Matt to say something, but all he did was hand her the money. After she counted out his change, he turned around and walked straight to a table.

Sarah's heart sank. She didn't expect him to comment that she was wearing the locket, but she had at least expected some conversation out of him. He usually chatted with her a little bit, even before they got to know each other. Today, he'd acted as though he didn't even know her.

She tried to think of what she'd done wrong. She couldn't think of anything she'd done to hurt his feelings, but obviously something had happened.

When he left, he didn't acknowledge her at all. He didn't even glance in her direction.

As soon as he was out the door, Sarah hurried to his table to see if he'd left her something—a note, his pen, anything. He hadn't.

She watched to see if he would hang around pretending to check his car while the other officer left. Matt's car drove off first.

All through the morning rush, all she could think of was Matt and what could be wrong. She couldn't think of a thing. By the time she left for class, she felt ready to burst into tears, which was totally unreasonable. From the first time she'd seen him away from work, she told herself that establishing a relationship was a bad idea, yet that was exactly what she'd done. She'd tried to fight it, but she felt herself falling for him, and now it was too late.

If she thought something had begun when he kissed her yesterday, judging from his actions today, the quickest relationship in history was over. The knowledge stabbed her heart where she didn't think she would heal.

Her eyes blurred as she slipped behind the wheel of her car. The engine roared to life as she turned the key. She waited a few seconds, and just as she slid the gearshift into reverse, a note under the windshield wiper caught her attention. She disengaged the shifter, yanked the parking break up, and scrambled outside to get the note.

Phone me when you get home. Short, sweet, and to the point, the note didn't have to be signed. She instantly recognized the meticulously neat handwriting. Even though whatever had barely started was over, at least now she would know why.

Fortunately, the morning classes demanded all her attention, so she didn't have to dwell on what would happen when she arrived home.

Once in the kitchen, she dumped her books and her purse in the middle of the table and dialed Matt's number.

It was obvious from his sleepy voice that she woke him up. She told herself not to feel guilty, because he had asked for her to call—she was only doing what she had been told to do.

"I'm glad you called. I wanted to let you know that I didn't mean to ignore you this morning."

Sarah tried to keep her voice from trembling. "Then why did you?"

"I thought it would be best if we don't give any indication that we've ever seen each other out of the donut shop. We can't do anything to arouse suspicion. As it is, more members are going to be dropping into Donnie's Donuts at varying times of the day and night. We're hoping Donnie doesn't notice. We don't want to make an issue of anything to do with members stopping in, and that especially includes fraternizing with the staff, more now than ever."

"Is that what this is? Fraternizing with the staff?"

"You know what I mean, Sarah. I shouldn't be seen talking to you, so I think it's a good idea to cut down on the chatter. We don't want to give anyone ideas."

"I guess."

"I'm worried about you. I hope you kept out of the closet today."

"I didn't go in the closet."

"While I'm talking to you, have you had any time to do any reading?"

"Not much."

He cleared his throat. "I was wondering. Wednesday night I go to a Bible study meeting if I'm not working. Would you like to come with me?"

"I thought you said we shouldn't be seen fraternizing."

A pause hung over the line. When he spoke, his voice came out softer and lower than usual. "I meant at Donnie's or in a public setting. But if you don't want to go with me, I'll understand."

Her heart pounded in her chest. She did want to go to learn more about the Bible. She also wanted to go with Matt.

"As long as I know far enough in advance to get enough sleep for work, yes, I'd like that. Did you say it was Wednesday night?"

"Yes. I'll pick you up at seven, and I can have you home by nine. Normally I'd ask if you wanted to go grab something for supper first, but I don't think we should be seen in a restaurant together. You never know who's watching, or who might recognize either one of us and let word slip back to Donnie. How about if I bring a pizza over to your place? But if you want to sleep, that's fine too."

The thought of his sneaking a pizza over so they wouldn't be seen together didn't appeal to Sarah. "I don't like sneaking around like this."

"I don't like it either, but we do have to be careful about where we go. I would think the small crowd at the Bible study meeting is safe, but I wouldn't trust being out in a public setting. You never know who you might see. I'm only being concerned for your safety and the integrity of the case."

Sarah's throat tightened. "How long do we have to keep this up?"

Once again, a silence hung on the line. "If we were only targeting locals, it would be a matter of days. But the department wants to go further up the food chain. Getting the evidence for a drug running operation can take years. I know that doesn't sound encouraging, but that's the way it goes."

A sinking feeling washed over her. She wanted to do what was good and right. She wanted to stop some of the drug trade and keep such evils way from the kids and teens and other adults too. But to have to keep up what Matt was suggesting would be grueling. She didn't want to hide, and she didn't like pretending not to know Matt when anyone might be watching them.

The good deed she had planned to do was no longer fun, and instead of being exciting, things had become frightening. Even so, she could live with simply keeping an eye on things while she was working, but for the situation to encroach on and limit her personal life was more of a sacrifice than she had planned.

She thought of some of the verses she'd read that day from the second chapter of James.

Suppose a brother or sister is without clothes and daily food. If one of you says to him, "Go, I wish you well; keep warm and well fed," but does nothing about his physical needs, what good is it?

She wanted to help stop the drug trade, but if she stood back and did nothing, what good was she doing?

Jesus wouldn't have wanted the children He loved harmed by illegal drugs.

"Yes, you're right. However long this takes to nail Kincaid and everyone that goes with him, then that's how long it's going to take. Pizza sounds good. I just hope I'm not sick of pizza by the time this is all over."

She could hear the smile in his voice as he replied. "It's not possible to get sick of pizza."

Sarah couldn't help but smile back. "Just like it's not possible to have too much coffee. I think you're in trouble, Matt. I'll see you Wednesday night."

fourteen

Sarah hummed to herself as she finished wiping up a table after a group of truckers. She was tired, but it was a good tired. Since their talk about not seeing one another in public, she'd already seen Matt twice. In private, of course.

He'd taken her to the Bible study meeting on Wednesday, which she had thoroughly enjoyed. He tended not to say much, but what he did say helped her to understand the lesson more clearly. Even though the time was short, she had enjoyed her time with him. The meeting had been held at the home of Gwen's twin brother, Garrett, and his wife Robbie. Sarah had known Garrett slightly when she was a teenager but lost touch when they all graduated. It was nice to see him again after all these years, as well as meet his wife and thereby expand her circle of friends. When she asked about why Gwen didn't go to her own brother's group, she discovered that Gwen and Lionel hosted their own home group on the same night.

Sarah had immediately liked Robbie, who was very friendly. Robbie had noticed the locket and asked to see the picture, just like Kristie had. When Sarah told her that she needed a picture of Matt to put in it, the whole group ganged up on him. Everyone chided Matt for giving a locket to a lady without a picture of himself in it. Sarah struggled not to laugh, knowing the real reason he'd given her the locket had nothing to do with a picture, and she watched him try to talk his way out of it, which was impossible.

To right an alleged wrong, Robbie brought out her digital camera and started snapping. One picture in particular of herself and Matt with their heads together hamming it up for the camera turned out very good. The best part was that when they reduced the picture to be small enough to fit into the locket, it was so small that their faces were virtually unrecognizable. Sarah now had a picture taped on top of the transmitter, so if anyone asked, she could now open the locket to show off her new "boyfriend," yet not have him be recognized.

The next time she'd seen Matt had been on Thursday afternoon. She'd stopped by Matt's townhouse to return his Bible, after finally getting the chance to go buy one of her own. This time she'd been inside his home, and, for the first time since she'd known him, she saw how he lived. If she hadn't seen it with her own eyes, she wouldn't have believed a man lived there. He hadn't been expecting her, yet his townhouse was perfectly clean; nothing was out of place, and everything was meticulously organized. While it did show a new side of his personality, it didn't surprise her. In or out of uniform, he was always perfectly dressed, with not a thread or a hair out of place. His car was also spotless inside, unlike hers, without a single paper, or napkin, spare book, or empty pop can rattling around in the back.

Now, due to his schedule, she probably wouldn't see him again until Monday.

As she made her rounds through the near-empty restaurant, Sarah carried the tray of cups and plates she was accumulating to the next table that needed cleaning. She had just started wiping when three surly men entered the building.

She thought the Ronsky clan looked like a rough bunch, but these men were older and had *gang* practically flashing in neon letters above their heads.

Instead of walking to the counter where Kristie was standing, they made a beeline straight to Sarah.

Sarah immediately grasped the locket and poised her finger on the release for the clasp. At this point in time, Matt was in bed sleeping, but he had told her to push the button any time, day or night, if she needed to. From the appearance of the men approaching her, Sarah feared this would be the time.

The tallest one, a shaved-bald man wearing a dirty denim jacket with torn-off sleeves over a T-shirt with a cigarette package tucked in the sleeve, stepped forward from the other two to address her.

"We need to see Donnie."

Sarah turned so fast her elbow knocked the tray. A few cups and plates crashed to the floor.

She forced herself to straighten to her full height. "I'll see if he's free. Can I have your names?"

The man gave her a horrid sneer. "Tell him Larry, Moe, and Curly Joe are here to see him."

A sick sensation rolled through Sarah's stomach. She didn't dare to challenge these men that those weren't their real names.

"Wait right here," she choked out and hurried to Donnie's office door, which was closed. She knocked. "Donnie?"

"Come in," he called out.

The door opened freely, indicating he hadn't locked it. Donnie sat behind his desk with a ledger book in front of him, his pencil in one hand, his other hand poised over the calculator.

"Three men are here to see you. They say their names are Larry, Moe, and Curly Joe."

Donnie's face paled. He cleared his throat. "Send them in. And leave the door open."

Sarah had barely taken one step out of Donnie's office when the three men barged past her, roughly shutting the door behind them.

Sarah glanced at the mess on the floor, then at Kristie, who was staring at Donnie's closed door with her mouth gaping open.

Sarah walked as quickly as she could without running to the opening between the restaurant and the kitchen. "I had better clean up that mess."

"You do that," Kristie mumbled, barely audible. "I'm going to stay right here."

As soon as she was out of Kristie's sight, Sarah ran for the closet. She slipped inside and closed the door, hoping Kristie really would stay where she was. Sarah dropped to her hands and knees and crawled to the corner of the closet, lowered her head to the level of the bottom shelf, and looked up through the vent.

Donnie was standing, his back to the wall, and the tall man with the shaved head stood mere inches from him.

Sarah grabbed the locket and opened it, her finger poised and ready to push the button, when she froze. Matt wouldn't come; it would be someone else, but that wasn't the point. The point of calling Matt, or any other police officer, was to bust the drug ring Blair Kincaid was involved in. If she pushed the button now, by the time the police arrived, she had no doubt that the three men would be long gone. The only thing to be accomplished would be to show Donnie that he was being watched, and that would defeat the purpose.

The man wasn't hurting Donnie, although he could have if he wanted to. Sarah suspected that his purpose was not to hurt, but to threaten. For that, she didn't need to call in the police.

Donnie's voice came out in a near squeak. "But I didn't go to him. He came to me."

"He's ours. Everything he gets is from us. Understand?"

Donnie's voice lowered. "What do you want me to do, ask for references first? He came to me. He had cash. So I gave it to him."

The tall man turned to the two others. After a few seconds of staring into each other's faces, the two men nodded.

"If he comes to you again, we get a cut. Do you understand what I'm saying?"

"I understand."

All three men turned at the same time. They all stepped to Donnie's desk. The hoodlum with the tattoo on his wrist knocked Donnie's calculator to the floor. Donnie remained with his back to the wall and said nothing.

Sarah didn't need to see any more. Their message was clear.

In two seconds, she'd backed up, grabbed the broom, and was out of the closet. She ran all the way to the point where Kristie could see her, then slowed her pace to a fast walk. She had just reached the broken glass when the door banged open and the three men walked out. The tall one pointedly turned in her direction, flashed the most evil smirk Sarah had ever seen, and walked straight out the door.

Sarah didn't know whether or not going in to Donnie's office to check on him would show she knew what happened, so she didn't. He was probably unhurt, but she didn't want to think of the condition of his office. Mentally, she tried to calculate how much damage could have been done between the time she grabbed the broom and when she arrived at the table.

Donnie appeared out of his office, quickly closing the door behind him. "If they ever come back, tell them I'm not here." He wiggled the doorknob and then joined Kristie behind the counter. "Kristie, I think it's time for you to start getting ready for the rush. I'll take over for you while Sarah cleans up."

Kristie obviously could take the hint because she disappeared in record time. Sarah lowered her head and began sweeping, afraid to look in Donnie's direction. She swept everything into the dustpan and carried it into the kitchen to dump in the garbage can.

With only a couple of people in the restaurant area, the building seemed unusually quiet. Sarah tried to shake off her apprehension, telling herself that since the three men were gone, everything would be fine. She stepped on the pedal to open the garbage can lid and was about to dump the broken glass when she heard the cash register drawer close.

Sarah froze. She hadn't heard any voices ordering anything, nor had she heard the shuffle of paper from donuts being selected, or the clink of the coffee pot, or the whirring of the latté machine.

She gritted her teeth. Knowing what she knew, she suspected that Donnie had just either taken money out of the till or put money in, although it was ridiculous because he was the owner and handled all the cash anyway.

She dumped the broken glass and let the lid thump closed. This time, when she opened the closet door, she turned the light on, banged around while she clipped the broom onto the hook, and closed the door loudly enough for Donnie to hear.

When she returned, he was standing at the donut rack. "Good, you're here. Take over. I'm going back into my office, and I don't want to be disturbed."

She suspected Donnie was cleaning up the mess and didn't want anyone to see what had happened.

By the time the morning rush had started, Donnie seemed back to normal, but Sarah couldn't relax. All through the busy morning, she kept one eye on the time. When she was done, she hurried out deliberately avoiding Kristie.

She had to leave a message for Matt, but for the first time, she was scared.

The creepy men had seen her up close, face-to-face. She knew she would recognize any one of them if she ever saw them again. Likewise, Sarah had no doubt they would recognize her too.

Because they knew she had witnessed them going into Donnie's office, she wondered if they might be watching her, in case she went to the police. They would have been right. Sarah had to report what she'd seen to Matt.

Just in case she was being followed, Sarah didn't drive to the police station to leave a message, as she'd done before. This time, she followed her usual route so no one could think anything was strange. Once on campus, she located the nearest phone booth and left a quick message at the police station for Matt to phone her. From the phone booth, she ran all the way to her first class, where she knew she would be safe.

❧

Matt stopped outside the parking area to the university and waited. As soon as he saw the little blue car, he began pursuit. He pushed the button for the siren to alert the car to stop, which it did.

"16Bravo4," he said to the radio.

"16Bravo4 copy," the dispatcher echoed.

"I'm out of service. I have a car pulled over, possible taillight infraction. Will advise."

"16Bravo4 copy."

Matt left his red and blue lights flashing and approached the driver's door of the little blue car.

"But officer, I wasn't speeding, I. . .Matt?"

"Hi, Sarah. I got your message. What's up?"

"What are you doing stopping me like this? I was on my way home. Where you were supposed to phone me."

"Didn't anyone ever tell you not to answer a question with a question?"

"Didn't your commanding officer or whatever you call him tell you not to scare people and not to pull them over for no reason?"

Matt grinned. Truthfully, he had been waiting for her to leave the parking lot. If she didn't notice him, he had planned to pull her over. When she turned out of the parking lot, he noticed she was missing a light, making this a legitimate stop. "Your driver's side taillight is out. I'm going to have to write you a warning to get it fixed."

She turned around and looked toward the rear of the car, which Matt thought ridiculous. Sitting behind the wheel, she couldn't see her taillights.

"You're kidding, right?"

"I'm serious. It's not a big deal. I have a package of bulbs at home I think will fit. What's up?"

"Something happened at Donnie's today. Three goons came to see him."

Matt stiffened. "Goons?"

She nodded so fast her hair bounced. "They were really sleazy looking characters. The one guy said their names were Larry, Moe, and Curly Joe." Her voice lowered. "But Curly Joe didn't have any hair. I don't know why he got that nickname."

A shiver of dread coursed through Matt. He knew exactly who they were. And no one messed with Curly Joe, shaved head or not.

Sarah grabbed her steering wheel with both hands. "They talked quite possessively about someone they knew going to Donnie, and it sounded like whoever it was bought some drugs from him. They said if it ever happened again, they wanted a cut. And then they started knocking things around Donnie's office." Her voice lowered. "They broke his calculator. On purpose."

Matt gritted his teeth and counted to ten. He forced himself to keep his voice low and even. "Those guys are bad news, and anyone can tell they're bad news just by looking at them. Why didn't you push the panic switch? How could you wait and only leave a message at the station? I told you to use it, any time, day or night."

"You told me that it was only to be used in an emergency, or when Kincaid was there with enough evidence to convict him. This was none of the above."

"If you couldn't tell, it sounds like they think Donnie is encroaching on their drug-selling territory, which could be true if Donnie is the new kid on the block. This isn't a game."

She rolled the window all the way down and stuck her head a little out the opening. "Maybe that's why I haven't seen Kincaid coming around until recently."

Matt shuffled closer to her. He rested his palms on the roof of her car and lowered his head in an effort to keep what they were saying private. People were starting to stare.

"While this new development is very interesting and proves that Donnie hasn't been at it very long, it doesn't negate the fact that you're in the middle of a very dangerous situation." He stopped talking and stared down at Sarah as she sat behind the wheel of her car. He replayed her words over in his head, trying to fit everything into place. Suddenly, he stiffened. An icy chill swept through him. "Just exactly how did you find out this information?"

She hunched her shoulders. "I heard them say it," she said softly.

"And how did you know they broke Donnie's calculator?"

"I. . ." Her voice trailed off. Matt's stomach clenched at the absence of a reply, which told him an answer he didn't want to hear.

Matt sucked in a deep breath in an effort to calm himself. "You were in the closet again!"

"You're shouting."

Matt backed up two steps. "That does it. Out of the car."

"Pardon me?"

Matt braced his feet apart, crossed his arms, and lowered his voice to a deep, even pitch. "You heard me. Get out of the car."

"What are you going to do, frisk me?"

He narrowed his eyes and glared at her.

Sarah's eyes opened wider than he'd ever seen them, and she looked back up at him. Very slowly, her door opened, and she inched out. As soon as both feet touched the ground and she stood upright, Matt unceremoniously escorted Sarah to the squad car.

"I can't believe this. What are you doing? It looks like you're arresting me!"

"I just might. You're not being a very cooperative criminal."

She stiffened, glanced down at his gun, then back to his face before she slid into the back seat of the squad car. Matt closed the door, then went around to the other side so he could get in as well. It really wasn't what he wanted to do, but he needed somewhere more private than the busy street where he could speak privately and not be under the watchful eye of every passerby.

"What were you doing in the closet?" he growled.

"You're still shouting at me. You may not be loud, but you're still shouting."

A few choice words raced through his head, but he held himself back. "I have every good reason to shout! I thought you agreed with me that it was too dangerous for you to be spying on Donnie when he's in his office! Do you have any idea of the risks you're taking?"

"Calm down. No one saw me or knew I was there. It's okay."

"It's not okay! All it takes is one slipup, and they could decide to make you a target to keep you silent. For good!"

"You're still shouting."

Matt lifted his hat off his head, swiped his fingers through his hair, and replaced the hat. "I'm sorry. But you're scaring me. You don't seem to realize the danger involved when you do stuff like that."

"I know the risks I'm taking. But I want to stop what's going on, and I can't if I don't know what Donnie is doing."

All he could do was stare at her. From the way she spoke, he did believe she really knew the risk she was taking, although perhaps not to the fullest degree. Then again, as a law enforcement officer, Matt had seen the worst cases played out in real life. He knew he'd been hardened to some degree by all he'd seen, but that didn't alter the facts. Worst-case scenarios did happen and nothing could assure him that this case wouldn't be one of them.

He didn't know what he would do if Sarah got hurt or worse. He didn't want to think about the danger she was putting herself in, but realistically, he had to. Her bravery only endeared her more to him. He had an almost overwhelming urge to kiss her, right in the back seat of his squad car. But he couldn't. He was in uniform, on duty, and out in public. It wouldn't have mattered if Sarah were his wife—people were always looking for any slipup any police officer made, in order to cause trouble or throw the department into disrepute.

He opened his mouth to say something, but nothing came out. He couldn't entertain the possibility of Sarah being his wife. He had already told himself that he would never marry a non-Christian, and he wasn't about to change his own rules. As a law enforcement officer, he knew it would be hard enough to maintain a happy, balanced marriage without adding more problems.

He wouldn't marry her, but nothing would stop him from caring about what happened to her. "Please promise me that you'll be more careful, and you won't go in the closet to spy on Donnie's office."

"I thought you wanted to catch Kincaid?"

"More than you'll ever know. But catching him isn't worth risking you."

"Since this whole thing began, I've had the feeling that this is very personal to you. Why do you want to catch this guy so badly?"

Matt turned and stared out the window, but his eyes didn't focus on anything in particular. "Kincaid was involved in a power game with a rival a few years ago. Kincaid has no respect for human life, and he only sees kids as easy marks or in the way. The end result was that one of my neighbor's kids found some of Kincaid's wares, didn't know what it was, and died from an unintentional overdose. Kincaid got off on a technicality and walked away laughing. I want to do everything I can to keep Kincaid off the streets, forever."

"I'm so sorry. Did you know the child well?"

Matt had to clear his throat in order to speak. "Yes. Her name was Jenni. She was only ten years old."

"That's so sad. . ."

He turned back to Sarah. Her concern was his final undoing. He couldn't kiss her on her warm, soft mouth, so he did the next best thing. He picked up her hand and kissed her palm. She gasped, but she didn't pull away. "I'm going to send you back to your car now. Please wait there while I write you up. All you have to do is come over to my place, and I'll give you a new lightbulb. I'll put in the report that I did the follow-up, and the file will be closed."

"This is silly."

"I know. But if anyone is watching, then there's something on file. I'll need your driver's license and registration."

Matt opened his door, walked around the vehicle, and opened the door for Sarah to get out. He followed her back to her car and waited for her to provide the documentation, then returned to the squad car and processed the warning.

He felt like an idiot, but if nothing else, it assured him that he would see her again in the next few days, before the warning expired, and he had to chase her down. Although doing a follow-up right now wasn't entirely a bad idea.

When everything was done, he returned to Sarah's window. He handed her the paperwork to sign, then tore off her copy and handed it to her.

She let go a loud sigh as she read the terms of the warning. "You're working tomorrow, aren't you?"

"Yes, but it's going to be a strange day. The RCMP has a booth in the mall this weekend for Bicycle Safety Week. I don't know what I did to deserve it, but I was assigned to do the booth. I'm stuck there from 10:00 A.M. until 6 P.M."

"Is that good or bad?"

"It's usually pretty boring, so it's bad. Give me a call when you want to change that lightbulb. And remember, Sarah. Please stay safe. No more trips to the closet."

fifteen

From a distance, Sarah watched the constable in the bright red RCMP serge uniform explain the proper way to wear a bicycle helmet. When the little girl was satisfied she knew how to wear her nice new pink helmet, he demonstrated to a group of boys what could happen to a head upon impact with the street at varying speeds. The demonstration turned out to be quite graphic, with pumpkins substituted for the heads.

Next, he handed brochures to a couple of teen boys who didn't appear to think it was very manly to wear helmets while on a bicycle. At the same time as they remarked on looking geeky, they kept glancing back to the mangled pumpkins that had started out with very realistic pictures of human faces.

Finally, when he was alone, Sarah approached the display booth.

"Good day, Constable Walker."

He touched the wide brim of his hat and gave her a slight nod. "Ma'am."

Sarah checked over her shoulder. Since no one was watching that she could tell, she shuffled up to a large map of the city park that highlighted a bike trail and rested one finger on what was described as a landmark. Matt stepped beside her.

"You sure look spiffy in your red serge," she said in a whisper just loud enough for him to hear.

He stiffened and clasped his hands behind his back, his trim physique making the uniform look even better. "Yeah, well, that's good, because it's not the most comfortable thing to wear. This collar is so high and done up so tight I can't turn my head properly. I've also gained a few pounds since I finished my training years ago, and it's a little more snug than it used to be."

Sarah tried not to giggle. He didn't know half the battle women had to face with their clothes every day. She didn't feel an ounce of sympathy for him. "Other than the uniform, how's it going?"

"As expected, I guess."

"It can't be all that bad."

He grinned from beneath the wide-brimmed hat. "Actually, it's kind of fun smashing those pumpkins."

"Men are just little boys who grew taller," she mumbled under her breath.

"Sorry, I didn't hear that. What did you say?"

"Nothing worth repeating. Are you allowed to take a lunch break? Or am I not allowed to be seen out in public with you?"

"Quite honestly, I don't think that's such a good idea here in the middle of the mall on a Saturday afternoon. Even though this is my full-dress uniform, I'm still in uniform, and I am officially on duty."

"Okay. Then tell me all about the bike trail at this park."

"What do you want to know? Do you really want to go mountain-biking or do you just want to make me talk?"

"I own a bike. I've never gone on a trail with it, but I do have one. It's packed in my storage closet in the underground parking. What about you?"

"Actually, I do a lot of biking."

"Do you go for distance or rough terrain riding?"

Matt grinned so brightly his eyes twinkled. "Rough terrain. I used to do BMX racing too, but the most biking I've been doing lately is taking my bike down to the Half-Pipe to do some skateboarding."

Sarah felt all the color drain from her face. "You mean those cement basins, where the kids go roaring up the sides, and do flips and stuff?"

Sarah wouldn't have thought it possible, but his grin widened even more. "It's okay. I always wear a helmet. And it's not only kids who do that, you know. The bigger guys just need better skateboards. And we have to go faster to get the height, but our weight helps the velocity. Still, I don't do it as much as I used to. Takes more out of me, I guess."

She wouldn't have taken him for a thrillseeker, but on second thought, it seemed to suit him. He had a dangerous job where he never knew what perils he would be facing from day-to-day, even hour-to-hour. At least with the extreme sports, the risks were obvious, and there were no surprises, although she knew there was always the possibility of injuries.

"I was right about men and little boys," she muttered, then cleared her throat. "If you're an avid biker, then maybe that's why they chose you to do the booth."

"Either that or everyone senior to me refused, and nobody junior to me is working this shift today."

"You have a bad attitude, do you know that?"

"I have a realistic attitude."

A mother and two boys stepped up to the display showing proper hand signals, so Sarah took that as her cue to leave.

Matt hadn't given her any indication if he would be back at the booth tomorrow, or if he was going to be back on regular duty.

Regardless of where Matt would be, Sarah knew where she was going tomorrow, and that was to church.

❧

Matt pulled into the entrance to his townhouse complex and steered down the hill toward his carport. He'd never been so glad to have a rotation end. He was dead-dog-tired, and he'd never needed to go home more in his life. On top of being at the end of the last twelve-hour shift, an armed robbery at a drugstore had kept him on an hour of overtime, and then he'd gotten stuck in the tail end of a traffic jam that resulted from an accident during the morning rush hour. At times like this, he wished he could reach forward, turn on flashing lights and a siren in his own car, and make the traffic part before him like Moses parted the Red Sea. Unfortunately, wishing wouldn't make it so.

The only thing that could possibly make him smile was

knowing that in forty-eight hours, he would be buzzing Sarah's apartment and taking her once again to a Bible study meeting.

As Matt rolled past the visitor parking, he blinked, slowed, and looked in the rear-view mirror.

Wishing hadn't made his own car have lights and sirens, but unless he was going crazy, wishing had made Sarah appear. Her car was sitting in one of the visitor parking stalls.

He was ready to hammer on the brakes and back up, but a movement in his driveway caught his eye.

It was Sarah.

Suddenly, Matt was no longer sleepy.

He accelerated slightly, steered into the carport, hit the brakes, and killed the motor. She walked up to the car and was ready, standing beside the door as soon as he got out. "Sarah? What are you doing here? Is something wrong?"

She smiled and held a small black rectangular object in the air at shoulder height. "No, something is very right! Look what I've got!"

She held the object out, and Matt accepted a small video cassette.

"What is this?"

"Have you got a camcorder you can hook up to your television? I hope so, because I don't. I want to see what's on this tape."

Matt waited for Sarah to elaborate, but she didn't. She merely stood behind him in silence as he unlocked his door and punched in the alarm code for his home security system. "It will take me a minute to hook everything up."

"No problem."

"Want to make us some tea or something?"

She turned toward the kitchen but didn't move. "I don't think so. Everything is so nice and clean, I hate to mess it up."

"How much mess could you possibly make?" He told her where to find the tea, a kettle, and the mugs, since he didn't own a teapot.

While Sarah remained in the kitchen to make the tea, Matt took his camcorder out of its case, removed the cables from the drawer, and began to connect the camcorder to the television. "By the way, why aren't you in class?" he called out.

He almost didn't want to hear the answer. If she was missing classes for the sake of the tape, it had to be something extremely important. The fact that she had the tape, yet didn't own a camcorder, made him all the more curious as to what it was.

The kettle whistled.

Sarah called her answer from the kitchen as she filled the cups with water. "The professor had an accident on the way to school, and there wasn't enough time to call in a substitute, so we got the morning off."

"I think I got caught in the traffic for that one. If it makes you feel any better, the victim looks like she has an excellent chance of recovery."

"That's great to know. Tomorrow we'll have a substitute, and we'll have to work extra hard to catch up, so I have to take advantage of today. That's why I'm here. I want a chance to see what's on that tape."

Matt's hand froze as he plugged the cable into the A/V jack. "If you don't know what's on this tape, then why are we going to watch it?"

"In case it's something good."

He was afraid to ask.

He turned on the television and set the camcorder to play. A crooked shot of a warehouse door opening appeared. A truck backed up, the driver and someone in a smock the same as Sarah's from Donnie's Donuts unloaded a few boxes, the truck drove off, and the door closed. The screen went blank.

Matt hit the pause button. "Well. That was certainly very interesting."

"I'm sure there's more. Put it back on."

The blank screen became alive again. Once more, the warehouse door opened, but a different truck backed in. The same man unloaded a few boxes with a different driver, the second truck drove off, the warehouse door closed, and the screen once more went blank.

"Okay. . ." Matt let his voice trail off. "I must be missing something. This isn't going to win any awards for interesting home videos."

"Be quiet and let's keep watching."

"If you don't mind, this time I'm going to fast forward it."

Two more trucks backed in, this time not taking so long to watch the process.

"That does it. What in the world is this?"

Sarah sipped the last of her tea and walked back into the kitchen for more hot water and a fresh tea bag. "It's the back door at Donnie's Donuts."

"I can see that. This doesn't appear to be an instructional video. The photography is quite bad, and it's crooked too. Plus it's in black and white. Where did you get this?"

"It's from a spy camera. You told me to keep an eye on things going in and out the back door, but I haven't seen anyone while I'm on night shift. So I put a hidden camera in the warehouse to watch what goes on at the back door during the daytime when I'm not there. It's got a motion detector, so it only goes on when something is moving. That's so it doesn't run out of film. Pretty cool, huh?"

Matt jumped to his feet and strode into the kitchen.

"You've got a spy camera set up at Donnie's Donuts?"

"Yes. Works pretty well, doesn't it? Let's keep watching until we see everything on the tape. I only have two tapes, so this one has to go back in the camera tonight. When can I give you the one that's in there today? Or maybe I should go buy a package of tapes, so we can watch them a few at a time."

Sarah lifted the mug and started to go around him on her way back to the living room. Matt blocked her path, removed the mug from her hand, and wrapped his fingers around her wrist. "Not so fast. I think you better go back to the beginning and explain this."

"I already told you. You said to keep an eye on—"

"I know what I told you. Let's have a little more detail."

"I put a spy camera in the loading area to catch what goes in and out the back door. It's really well hidden. It's made to look like a cheap air freshener, so I put it near the door on top of a bunch of junk that no one has touched for the last year. No one will even notice it. At night it's no problem for me to quickly switch tapes and the battery pack, and it's good for another day." One side of her mouth quirked down. "I just don't know what I'm going to do about the weekends. Although with fewer deliveries, there would be less movement. So if there's anything going through the back door, it would be bad guys, right?"

Matt shook his head. "Where in the world did you get surveillance equipment?"

She smiled so brightly her entire face lit up. "e-Bay! You wouldn't believe what they've got on there. There was another surveillance system that was a teddy bear, but I think they would have noticed that, so I bought the air freshener one instead."

"You've got to be kidding. . ."

"No, I'm not. It was really cheap too. The ad said some cables were missing and some kind of switch was broken. So I took it to the audio-video department at the university, and some really nice guys fixed it for me. They even gave me the missing wires for free!"

Matt squeezed his eyes shut. Detective Cunningham was very much on duty. Unfortunately.

"Sarah, you can't do that."

"Why not? I know you can't use stuff like that in court, but at least you would be able to see the thugs Donnie is dealing with. Then you guys can do whatever it is you do to catch drug dealers."

"What if someone finds it and discovers what it is?"

"If any of the staff found it, they would think Donnie put it there. They'd just put it back, behave really nice around it, and not admit to Donnie that they found it. If someone throws it ut because the air freshener doesn't work, that would be a shame, but I didn't pay much for it, so I wouldn't cry about it or anything. Although I doubt I'd ever find another one at such a good price."

"For your information, we've already spotted some suspicious characters known to the police lurking around the back door of Donnie's. We're keeping tabs on them just fine, without you being a super-spy."

"But they're not watching the back door twenty-four/seven, are they?"

"No. We don't have a budget for that yet, until we can determine something really big is going on. For now, all we have is suspicion and the fact that you've witnessed a few things go through. But compared to the big picture, what you've seen isn't a lot. We've got to find more."

"I know that. That's why I got the spy camera." She straightened, set her shoulders back, and smiled as if she was extremely proud of herself.

"Let's sit down in the living room. We have to talk."

He released her hand, allowing her to pick up her mug of tea. Matt escorted her back into the living room, where they sat side by side on the couch. "The drug trade is really serious business. If drug dealers think someone has crossed them, or even think someone is going to, they have no hesitation in bumping them off. To them, life is cheap. I don't want you getting involved in this."

"Don't you see? If I can help the police find out the crook Donnie is dealing with, then this whole thing will be over so much faster, and then there will be less chance of anyone finding out anything about me. I don't want this to go on for years. I want my life back."

Matt couldn't agree more. He wanted so much to get to know Sarah better, to involve her in all parts of his life, which meant taking her to church on Sunday and spending more time with her. He found it very encouraging that she'd borrowed his Bible.

He didn't know why she'd borrowed it, but he would do every
thing he could to help her discover Jesus for herself. When h
couldn't take her to church on Sunday, he was doing the nex
best thing by taking her to the meetings Wednesday night
Then, if she had any questions that he didn't know the answer t
she would be with people who would.

Having to restrict his contact with her hurt, especially now
He felt safe taking her to a small home group but not the publi
setting of church. On an occasional Sunday, he actually saw
people he'd arrested for various offences. Going to church didn
instantly erase dishonesty. In the big picture, it meant there wer
questionable characters in church sitting alongside the saint
The risk of someone seeing Sarah at church with a known co
was always present. Therefore, he would continue to go t
church alone.

For now, it didn't matter, anyway. With the rotation changing
only by one day each week, he hadn't been to church for th
past two weeks, and he wouldn't be able to go for two more.

He turned toward the television, which had been on paus
for so long the tape had clicked off.

He'd experienced the evidence-gathering process for dru
rings before. Sometimes they dragged on forever. Even thoug
Sarah's videos wouldn't be admissible in court, it was perfectl
fine and legal to post the potential perps on the bulletin board
That way, they could identify them as potential perps for rea
surveillance away from Donnie's. If allowing Sarah to make th
tapes would speed up the case, he had to trust her when sh
said she knew what she was doing and would be perfectly safe.

He took a deep sigh. "Okay, you win. Make your tapes. Bu
remember, if there is any chance that someone might see you
even if it means missing a day or two, or even more, then ski
those days. My only concern is your safety. The case can dra
on all it wants, as long as you're safe."

Her bright smile nearly lit the room. "Deal. Now let's watc
the rest of this tape, and then I'll go home and let you ge

ome sleep. You look really tired."

Matt picked up the remote and fast-forwarded through the
ape as they watched. The same warehouse door went up and
own more times than he wanted to count. Nothing of any note
appened, so Sarah rewound the tape, and tucked it in her purse.

"I guess this means I'll see you tomorrow. Is noonish okay?"

"Noonish?"

"If that doesn't work, we can pick another time. It would be
ice if we could just pick the same time every day, but your
hifts don't allow that."

Her words rolled over in his head. *Every day.* Her little spy
mission with the hidden camera meant that he would be seeing
Sarah every day as they watched the back door together.

He couldn't tamp down his smile. Perhaps Detective
Cunningham was onto something after all.

sixteen

"Matt, wait for a minute. I need to talk to you."

Matt turned around and stepped back into the room after the last of the other members left for their squad cars.

The debriefing had gone well. In the four days he'd been on Sarah's hidden camera had come up with a few faces at the back door who weren't delivering groceries. They'd moved the cam corder hookup from his television to his computer and capture a few stills. They now had grainy but recognizable prints of number of suspects going out with what Donnie was bringing i. They couldn't use the pictures in court, but they had somethir to show the other members as to whom they should be on th watch out for.

Researching what was coming in to Donnie was beyon Matt's ability to investigate. Moving Sarah's spy camera into th closet to keep tabs on Donnie's office would show only the pas ing of drugs and money from Kincaid to Donnie, which the already knew about. Therefore, he'd convinced her to keep th camera where it was. They needed to know where Kincaid supply came from, and no camera or inside spying was going answer that question. He had to trust the department to tak care of what was coming in.

Most of all, keeping the camera at the back door kept Sara out of the closet.

"What's up, Jeff?"

"That informant of yours is really something."

Matt forced himself to keep a straight face. "Yeah, she really is."

"Your report didn't say if she's seen Kincaid recently or ho often or regularly Kincaid comes in."

All traces of any reason for smiling disintegrated. Sara

uld readily find out how often Kincaid came in by moving
e camera, but that meant she would be putting herself at risk
ith the closet.

"You don't really need to know that, do you? Me telling you the
xt day that Kincaid was in isn't going to help find out his sup-
ier. Nor is it going to tell you who else Kincaid is selling to."

"You seem to be pretty tight with your informant. I was just
ondering if she had a way of finding out any more. We have
know where he's going, but we don't have the budget we
ed for all the surveillance."

"I think you're pushing it, Jeff. She's just a counter clerk, and
regular upright citizen. She only found out about Kincaid by
cident and was civic minded enough to tell the police. That's
e only reason I became involved with her."

"I wonder. . ."

Matt's gut clenched. He'd just admitted to his superior officer
at he was involved with Sarah, although he hadn't said exactly
ow personally involved he was. If they knew, they would have
m immediately pulled off the case because personal feelings
uld affect an officer's judgment. However, he was in too deep
back off. To any other member, she was simply an informant,
lling to take a little risk. But to Matt, she was. . .he wasn't
ite sure, but he was sure enough not to let her go.

"I know she's done a lot of work for a civilian, but she's doing
lot of it for me because I think she likes me. I don't know if
e'd get this involved if she was working with anyone else
cause as you say, there is an element of risk involved."

Jeff frowned. "That does muddy the waters, somewhat,
esn't it?"

Jeff had no idea how much it muddied the waters.

"Well, okay. I guess I'll have to let it go."

"There's possibly one thing I could get her to do. But we
ave to make a deal."

Jeff's eyebrows raised, and he blatantly stared at Matt, proba-
y unable to believe a junior officer would be bargaining with

his superior. But that was exactly what Matt was doing.

"I might be able to get her to signal me, to let me kn⟨
when Kincaid walks in the door. If she can, I have to be assur⟨
that no member will be anywhere in sight. An undercover ⟨
can follow Kincaid from Donnie's Donuts and see where h⟨
going, and that's it. I don't want any surveillance operation ⟨
be associated with Donnie's Donuts. Besides Donnie himse⟨
there are only two women working there at night. Kinca⟨
would think nothing of having one or both of them terminat⟨
if he thought that's where the trouble was starting."

"I could probably live with that. It's better than wha⟨
happening now. We can't seem to find Kincaid when he's ⟨
to something, so this would be a good start. Donnie's Donu⟨
is probably his first delivery because he's dropping off ca⟨
when he makes his rounds."

Matt shook his head. "I think Donnie's is his last drop-⟨
because he's collecting the cash as he goes."

"I don't think Kincaid would take cash from one drop-off ⟨
another, in case he gets bumped for it. Donnie's is his first stop⟨

Both men stared at each other in silence.

Matt dragged one hand down his face. "The bottom line ⟨
we really don't know. Give me a few days to think about it, a⟨
I'll discuss it with her, but no promises. I gotta get going, n⟨
calls are backing up."

Matt hurried out to his squad car, where for another day, ⟨
would simply be "16Bravo4," facing a typical Saturday ⟨
shoplifters, speeding tickets, and following up on his breaki⟨
and entering and theft files. Between that, he would simp⟨
cruise around to show the colors, which told people the RCM⟨
was on duty in their neighborhood, and to make his presen⟨
known enough so that at least some of the bad guys wou⟨
behave for a while. As he and all the other members had be⟨
instructed, he stopped for his break at Donnie's Donuts. It fe⟨
different, even wrong, not seeing Sarah there.

But when he got off work that evening, Sarah was comin⟨

er for dinner. The thought made the whole day worthwhile.

❧

arah pushed the doorbell to Matt's townhouse. When he
lled for her to come in, the delicious aroma of a pot roast
afted up to her the second she opened the door.

Sarah smiled. Apparently, Matt enjoyed cooking for her as
uch as she enjoyed cooking for him. Either that or he was
ying to one-up her after the honey baked honeyed ham she'd
ade for him on the weekend.

She immediately walked to the kitchen and smiled at the
ght of him. He looked bigger than ever in the kitchen, lean-
g over the open oven door, a dishtowel slung over one
oulder, oven mitts on his hands, as he gently set a roasting
n on the stovetop.

"Constable Walker, you are going to make me fat."

"I doubt that."

"It's true. I've put on a pound and a half in the past two
eeks since you've been cooking for me."

"That's not my fault. I've been cooking good, healthy dinners.
s your cooking that's putting any weight on because you make
sserts and I don't." He smiled as he patted his stomach with
e still-mitted hand. "Although I have to admit, I sure do enjoy
ssert, and I'm not going to turn you down. I also couldn't help
t notice that you brought donuts with you again today."

She grinned back, placing one hand on her own stomach
st as Matt had done. "Sorry. Staff discount."

While Matt sliced the roast, Sarah set the table and poured
vo glasses of milk. They worked together to put all the food
n the table, said a prayer of thanks, and began to eat.

As hungry as she was, Sarah only took one bite and began
toy with a piece of roasted carrot. "Something strange hap-
ened today, and it's really bothering me."

Matt stabbed a potato, and ate it. "What?"

"Kincaid came in with another duffel bag. It felt really
eepy, knowing what was in it. Anyway, later in the night, I

was in the kitchen, and I dropped a knife between the count
and the donut cooker. I was almost all the way underneat
when I heard Donnie walk into the kitchen. He kept check
ing over his shoulder like he didn't want anyone seeing wh
he was doing, then he took a bag of icing sugar out of th
cupboard and into his office. He closed the door, and he w
in there a long time. He looked really guilty, like he was stea
ing it or something. Do you think he's hiding drugs in th
kitchen supplies? What if drugs get used in the donuts, ar
customers eat them?"

"He's not hiding drugs in it. He's using the icing sugar to cut th
coke he's selling. Happens all the time. What people buy on th
street is nowhere near the purity of how it comes in. Donnie
adding the icing sugar to increase the volume before he sells it."

"That's so dishonest!"

Matt froze, his fork in midair. "Sarah. Think about what yo
just said. He's dealing drugs. He's not being honest to begin with.

She felt her cheeks heat up. "Oops. I guess that was kind
stupid, wasn't it?"

He smiled so sweetly she instantly felt better. "Not stupid.
wish we had more criminals as honest as you. Actually, it's
good thing you mentioned Kincaid going into Donnie'
There's something I need to talk to you about."

She immediately covered her heart with one hand and raised th
other palm in the air. "I never went in the closet! I promise! Kinca
just came in, and I stayed behind the counter the whole time."

"It's not that. My staff sergeant asked if there's some way yo
can notify us when Kincaid arrives. They want an undercov
unit to follow Kincaid after he leaves Donnie's Donuts. I did
tell him about the transmitter I gave you, but I did tell him we
discuss it."

"I don't understand."

"On nights when I'm working, if Kincaid comes in, wou
you be able to signal me? In turn, I can radio dispatch. If the
have someone in the area who's available, they can tail Kincai

not, then they would wait until next time."

"But you said only to press the button in case of an emergency."

"I know. I was thinking about that. It would take longer if emergency happened, so it's up to you to decide if you want do this. The receiver vibrates for fifteen seconds, then stops. ꞁe signal would be to buzz once if Kincaid comes in. If it's emergency, after you hit the button, count out twenty sec-ꞁds, then hit it again. If it vibrates twice, then I'd know it was emergency."

"I don't see a problem with that."

"But that would mean notifying me of an emergency would ꞁe an extra twenty seconds."

She shrugged her shoulders. "What's twenty seconds?"

"In a life-and-death situation, you'd be surprised. After you ꞁhale, without taking a deep breath first, hold your breath for ꞁenty seconds. You'll see how long it is."

Following instructions, Sarah did exactly as she was told. She ꞁdn't last fifteen seconds before she had to inhale. "That's scary. ꞁvasn't even moving. I'm just sitting down, relaxing."

"That's right. Think about what I said and let me know ꞁmorrow."

"Okay. Tomorrow is Bible study meeting night. Are we going?"

"You bet."

After dinner, Sarah helped Matt do the dishes and get ꞁerything put away. Matt froze a frame from the tape of the ꞁy and pulled out a picture of yet another person who had ꞁme to buy drugs from Donnie.

She'd never thought about Donnie being at the donut shop ꞁuring the daytime because he was there for the entire night ꞁift. However, watching the tapes proved he was there during ꞁe daytime too. Sarah wondered if the day shift staff knew ꞁat Donnie was there at night.

When Matt hit *print,* he turned around in his chair. ꞁVhen we finally do bust the place, now I know why he's ꞁere so long. Working from the donut shop lessens the

chance of being caught with any drugs on his person. H
accepts it at the front door, cuts it in his office, and sells
straight out the back door. He's got quite a little operatio
going there." Matt grinned. "Too bad we're going to be shu
ting him down soon."

Matt rewound the tape and gave it to Sarah. She tucked tl
tape into her purse. "I won't be here until later tomorrow. I'
going to go to bed soon after I get home. I'll set my alarm sc
can be awake when you come to watch the tape, and then we
go to the meeting."

"Sounds good to me."

As usual, Matt walked with her to the door, but this time, inste;
of opening it for her, he rested his hands on her shoulders.

"This is getting so complicated. I worry about you." H
hand remained on her shoulders as he nudged the bottom
her chin on both sides with his thumbs.

"I know you do. I'm being really careful, and I'm staying out
the closet. You've got no need to worry. But I worry about you."

One side of his mouth quirked up in a lopsided smile. "M
You don't have to worry about me."

She raised her hands and rested her palms on his chest. Sl
felt the steady, even beat of his heart beneath her hands. "Yc
do dangerous things all the time. It's your job to go chasir
criminals and investigating things when you don't kno
what's lying in wait around the corner. You go speedir
through traffic and never know if someone's going to run tl
red light or you're going to hit something because you'
going so fast. Of course I have to worry about you."

His smile dropped. "I don't know what to say. No one h;
ever worried about me before."

Beneath her palms, his heartbeat quickened. At the sam
time, he cupped her cheeks with his hands.

Sarah closed her eyes. Matt was going to kiss her, and sl
wanted to kiss him too.

His kiss was sweeter than the donuts she'd brought f

ter dinner. His mouth lifted only long enough for him to
hisper her name, then he kissed her again. When she
ought they were going to separate, he dropped his hands
om her cheeks to around her back. Sarah barely had time to
ll her hands out from between them before he pulled her
oser, embracing her fully. She wrapped her arms around his
ck and sank into his warm, hard chest. Matt rested his
eek on the hair on top of her head.

While being held felt better than she could ever describe,
e knew what they were doing wasn't smart, but she couldn't
and by and do nothing. The drug trade hurt children, as well
adults, and she had to do whatever she could to make a dent
it, even though she knew she would never stop it.

The more she read in her Bible, the more she thought
at nothing happened by accident. The opportunity to do
mething had been dropped into her lap for a reason. If
sus were watching, He knew she couldn't stand by and do
othing. Regardless of the danger or risk, Sarah had to see
to the end.

Yet, the situation between her and Matt was even scarier
an any predicament she found herself in at Donnie's
onuts. Matt was a cop, and he did a dangerous job every
y. Even Matt's choice of leisure activities carried consider-
le risk.

She couldn't help it. She liked him. A lot. Being wrapped
the protection of his arms only made it worse.

He shuffled, making Sarah think he was going to kiss her
ain. Just as he started to move his hands, the phone rang,
using him to flinch.

"The answering machine will get it," he muttered into her
ir.

Matt's voice came over the speaker with a brief ditty to wait
r the beep and start talking.

"Matt, it's your mother. Pick up the phone. I've got some-
ing to tell you."

Matt sighed and moved away. "I had better get that. Excuse me
Sarah moved all the way to the door. "Don't worry about
Talk to your mother. I'll let myself out. See you tomorrow."

seventeen

Sarah smiled as she placed the latest tray of fresh donuts into the display case. She couldn't remember ever being so tired. She didn't know how she was going to make it through school and still keep her eyes open, but today had been the best day of her life.

On Wednesday, Matt had been on nightshift, so he couldn't go with her to the Bible study meeting. Therefore, she'd gone without him. During the meeting, someone had asked a question about Jesus that had turned the whole topic of the study around. Listening to the discussion, something inside her clicked. She'd already known Jesus was real and that He had lived just as the Bible said He did. But suddenly, she felt the love He offered to her as an individual person, instead of as just one part of a faceless crowd of people.

She had so many questions she didn't know where to start, so she'd waited until the next day. Since Matt would have been sleeping after a hard day, she'd phoned Pastor Colin and gone down to the church office. There, she'd asked all her questions, and Pastor Colin prayed with her to receive Jesus into her heart. Now, she truly was a child of Jesus.

Pastor Colin first phoned his wife. Then he invited Sarah to his house for supper, which she accepted because she was too excited to sleep. She'd managed to have a short nap before she ran out the door for work, but now, halfway through the night, the lack of sleep was catching up with her. She was tired, but at least it was a happy tired.

Sarah's smile widened as she realized she was humming a song she'd learned in church from the previous Sunday. Next Sunday, Matt would finally be able to attend church after having to work four Sundays in a row. He would be pleased that she now knew so many songs. That was, if he thought it was a good idea to sit together, because he considered church a public setting.

It didn't matter. If she had to sit alone or with Gwen and Lionel again, Sarah didn't care. She was going to church to worship God, not to sit with Matt.

Behind her, the main door opened. Sarah tucked the last of the donuts neatly into the row, and turned to serve the customer who just walked in.

All traces of her smile dissolved. She forced herself to smile politely, even though it hurt, as she stared up into the face of Blair Kincaid. No duffel strap crossed his shoulder. Sarah quickly glanced down to his hand and back to his face.

He was carrying a briefcase. The briefcase.

He smiled and looked pointedly at her nametag, then back to her face. "Hi, Sarah. May I see Donnie? I know he's here."

Sarah turned her head briefly toward Donnie's door, which was closed. "I'll see if he's available," she choked out.

She walked as slowly as she could to Donnie's office, in order to stretch out the time. The second her back was fully to Kincaid as she neared the door, she reached up with one hand, flicked the locket open, pushed the button, and snapped the locket shut. She felt little satisfaction at how efficiently she worked the locket and button with one hand. All she felt was fear.

If the police did manage to send someone within five minutes, the amount of time she knew Kincaid would be there, she prayed he wouldn't discover he was being followed. Besides Donnie, Sarah was the only person who knew Kincaid was there.

Once she had the locket snapped shut, she knocked on Donnie's door. "Donnie? Someone's here to see you."

"Send him in." She found it interesting that Donnie knew the visitor was a "him" and singular.

To make the process take longer, Sarah closed the door, and returned slowly to the counter. Back behind the cash register, she faced Kincaid, who was no longer smiling. "Would you like a cup of our special vanilla latté before you go see Donnie? It's half price today."

His smiled returned, and he reached for his back pocket. "Sure, that sounds good."

Sarah took his money first, then pretended the cups were stuck together before she placed one into the machine and pressed the button. She remained with her back turned to Kincaid until the very last drop dripped out. Without taking her hand off the cup as she slid it across the counter to him, she looked up and again forced herself to smile. "Do you have a Donut Dollars card? After you buy ten lattés, you get the next one free. That's a really good deal, especially when they're half price."

He smiled again, but he still looked as ugly and evil as ever. "Sure, I'll have a Donut Dollars card."

In slow motion, Sarah removed a card from the bundle, purposely dropped the stamp on the floor, then pretended the snap-on lid wasn't snapping off very easily. She made a great show of putting the stamp in exactly the right position, and held up the card for him to see. "Here you go. Enjoy the latté." If it weren't cold by now.

He smiled at her one more time, then turned, and walked into Donnie's office.

❧

Matt groaned as he rolled over in the bed and reached for the phone. When he put it to his ear and mumbled a sleepy "hello," dial tone buzzed in his ear, and the ringing continued.

In a flash, Matt sat up on the bed. The clock radio glowed 3:47 A.M. The ringing was coming from the receiver to the transmitter in Sarah's locket.

He held the phone to catch some of the light coming in from between the curtains and dialed the private number the members used to call into the station.

"This is Constable Matt Walker. I need dispatch."

The line clicked and was picked up in two rings. "Please state your emergency," the voice answered.

The receiver stopped ringing.

"Joan, it's Constable Matt Walker. Something's happening at Donnie's Donuts. Hang on for a sec."

With his heart banging in his chest, Matt counted to five. Nothing. He waited another five seconds. No second ring.

He sagged with relief then spoke into the phone. "Blair Kincaid just walked in at Donnie's Donuts. Send out a plain car right away."

"Copy. Stay on the line."

A click sounded, and the canned music started. Matt sat frozen in one spot, forcing himself to breathe evenly.

He prayed for Sarah every day. For an awakening of her faith. That she'd do well on her next test. Sometimes he even prayed she'd get to work on time without speeding. While he waited, he blocked out the music and did something he also did every day— he prayed for her safety, then that a member could arrive before Kincaid left, and Kincaid wouldn't figure out he was being tailed.

The music went dead, and Joan's voice came back on the line. "Unit dispatched ETA six minutes."

"16Bravo4 copy." He smiled when he heard Joan's giggle. "I meant just copy. Thanks Joan."

His smile dropped when he hung up the phone. If it took that long for a unit to arrive, it would be close, if not too late. For today, both he and Sarah had done their best; he could only hope and pray that it worked.

Matt knew he would never be able to fall back to sleep, so he got dressed, clipped the receiver onto his belt, set the mode to vibrate, and went into the living room to read. If she buzzed again, he would be at Donnie's Donuts in eight minutes, lights and sirens or not. But for now, he had to stay put.

He wanted to do something to burn off his nervous energy. His first thought was to shoot some hoops, but the bouncing basketball would have made too much noise at four in the morning. Besides, he needed to stay close to the phone, in case Sarah called.

After half an hour of frustration, Matt calmed himself down enough to quit pacing. He settled into the couch and read all the

:tions in his Bible he had marked about anxiety and worry.

After an hour of reading, he thought he could finally go
:ck to sleep.

But first, he set the alarm for noon. If Sarah hadn't shown
> by twelve-thirty with the tape of the day, he knew where he
.s going.

ঞ

att snatched up the phone within one ring.

Sarah's excited voice came over the line. "Did you catch him?"

He sighed. "It's not like someone went chasing after Kincaid
:th lights and sirens. If they got there in time, they simply fol-
wed him to see where he was going. Hopefully, he went some-
1ere worthwhile. I won't know officially what happened until I
> back to work on Monday." Although since he was the officer
 charge of keeping tabs of what went in and out of Donnie's
:onuts, a quick phone call to Jeff, even on his days off, would
.ll him what he needed to know. By now, whoever tailed
.incaid would have their report in the computer.

A pause hung on the line. When Sarah finally spoke, her
·ice came out low pitched and husky. The airiness made Matt's
:art pound. "I wanted to tell you how much I appreciate the
·ay you're looking out for me. Knowing what's going on has
:en scary. If it wasn't for you and being able to contact you at
.e push of a button, I think I'd be in the insane asylum by now.
 really am a chicken, but knowing you're there gives me
rength and courage I didn't know I had. Thank you."

Matt opened his mouth, but no sound came out. Sarah was
.uch stronger than she knew. He'd seen it in her character all
·ong, which was probably one of the reasons he'd fallen
 love with her so quickly. She was strong in so many ways.
he needed just a little push to bring her to her full potential.
he was motivated and persistent, possessing levels of
1durance he seldom saw, to keep up with her demanding
:hedule to work full-time and attend college classes half-
me. Yet she still managed to see him nearly every day, and

she'd only fallen asleep on the couch once. Those same qu—
ties would have made her a good cop, if she were taller —
stronger. Her main goal in life, being a teacher of small ch—
dren, was another challenge. It required courage and stam—
of a different kind, but she had it.

She held his heart in the palm of her hand, and he w—
powerless to resist.

He cleared his throat when he was finally able to spe—
"Where are you?"

"I'm at home. I'm so tired I can't think straight. I have to
to sleep."

"When do you think you'll be here so we can watch the tape?"

"Would seven work for you?"

"Seven is fine. See you then."

In slow motion, Matt hung up the phone. He'd nearly los—
and told Sarah he loved her. He'd been fighting it for weeks, —
this final bit of pressure and her words today sealed the proc—
and pushed him over the edge. He was hopelessly in love w—
her, and there was nothing he could do.

Yet, as a cop, he was well aware of how fear and pressu—
especially in a possibly life-threatening position created an a—
ficial emotional dependency. Since he'd had no indication fr—
Sarah that the connection he wanted went both ways in a n—
mal setting, he could only conclude that when he kissed h—
her response had been under duress and not to be construed —
real or permanent. She saw him as the source of her streng—
and he wasn't. He was just an ordinary guy with an extraor—
nary job. He was a cop, and it was his job to show strength.

Matt buried his face in his hands. He should be going in —
talk to Jeff and have himself pulled off the case, but he could—
He was in too deep, and there was no way out. Regardless —
the fact that she didn't feel the same way as he did, she trust—
him to take care of her, and he was responsible for her.

Worse, he trusted his fellow officers with his own life, —
he didn't trust them with Sarah's.

Matt stood and strode into the kitchen. After another
ghtening episode, he knew what would calm her, and that
as a good dinner.

It was a good thing tonight was his turn to cook because he
anned to give her a meal she'd never forget.

eighteen

Sarah hit the button to open the main door, then set the sc
loped potatoes on the table. She could tell when Matt phoned
tell her that he was going to be late that he'd had a bad day. S
was glad she told him that today she would do the cooking si
he was on day shift.

She smiled as she sliced the meatloaf. The dinner she m
today paled in comparison to Matt's cooking. One day l
week, he'd made a stew with dumplings like none other sh
had in her life. He'd told her that he didn't know how much
enjoyed cooking until she came into his life.

Sarah didn't know if that was a good thing or not, because
much as she enjoyed it too, her pants didn't fit like they used to.

She'd already unlocked the door when he buzzed, allowi
him to come right in after he knocked. He immediately flopp
down at the table.

"What a day. I'm just wiped. That smells good. Can I
anything?"

"Yes." Sarah set the meatloaf on the table and joined hi
"You can pray."

Matt froze for a second, tipped his head slightly, and look
at her. He didn't say anything, but she thought a smile flit
across his face before he quickly bowed his head. He cleared
throat, said a short but heartfelt prayer of thanks, and th
immediately dug into the food.

"I don't want to wreck this meal, but I have to talk to you ab
something. There's something strange happening at Donni
Stranger than usual. Kincaid walked in, this time, instead
trying to charm me, he barged straight into Donnie's office. I
sorry. I couldn't help myself. I went into the closet."

"Sarah. . ."

She waved one hand in the air. "Don't interrupt me. Kincaid said he's noticed the place has been crawling with cops lately. Donnie told him he heard about some kind of donut-eating contest you guys are doing."

Matt grinned from ear to ear. "Yeah. The contest was Ty's idea. He named it, 'A Donut a Day.' Everyone in the department stops in to Donnie's once a shift to buy a donut. It's an elimination game based on the pick of the day. I won last round."

Sarah tried her best to give him a dirty look, but he didn't take the hint. "Donnie assured Kincaid that no one had any idea what was going on. So it's bad that Kincaid noticed, but it's good that Donnie isn't taking it seriously. But then, Kincaid suddenly got really serious and accused Donnie of skimming some of the money, and they started arguing."

All traces of Matt's smile disappeared. "That happens. You have to understand that when people are laundering money, there is no paper trail. When you have two people who each want their share of sums of money, and everything is verbal, they often don't come up with the same figures when the day is done. Add money for drug sales going in and out of an amount that hasn't been written down, and you're asking for trouble. I was wondering how long it was going to take that to happen."

"So Donnie's stealing already stolen money?"

"Or Kincaid wants more than originally agreed. As well, since this is drugs and drug money they're dealing with, one or both of them could be taking free samples, which further clouds judgment and the ability to remember numbers."

"This is really bad, isn't it?"

Matt shrugged his shoulders. "It's good for us, because this is where they can get sloppy. But it's bad for you, because you're right there. I want you to stay clear of those guys when they get together. Whatever you do, don't take sides, even in something as simple as comments about the weather."

"But Donnie is my boss!"

"I know. I wish there was something I could do. We think we've found out where Kincaid is getting his supplies, but we have a few more names to check and a few holes in the supply chain. It looks like the end is getting nearer. But until then, I want you to stay away from them, and—"

Sarah held up her hands to cut him off. "I know. And stay out of the closet."

❧

Sarah grumbled to herself as she swept up the litter around the table the Ronsky clan had just deserted. She had just swept everything into one pile when the front door opened. Kincaid burst in, a duffel bag slung over his shoulder. This time he didn't even look at her or ask permission. He headed straight for Donnie's office.

Remembering Matt's statement that their information was still incomplete, Sarah reached up to the locket and pushed the button.

Donnie's door slammed shut. Raised voices echoed through the door, but not of a volume where Sarah could understand what was being said.

Kristie appeared beside her. "I don't know what's been going on around here, but something's not right. That guy seems to come in at the strangest times, and I just don't like him."

"I know what you mean," Sarah mumbled. "I think it might be a good idea to go behind the counter and stay there until it's over."

Sarah looked up at the time. She'd buzzed Matt a number of different times when Kincaid walked in. The last time she'd buzzed, the police hadn't made it with an undercover person in time to follow Kincaid. Even though she was becoming increasingly nervous about the situation, she wished there were something she could do to make Kincaid stay longer, so the police had more time to get there. However, last night Matt had warned her to keep her distance. Seeing the foul look on Kincaid's face today, that seemed like excellent advice, and Sarah fully intended to take it.

She handed the dustpan to Kristie. "Hold this, and we can

both get out of here in a few—"

The front door banged open. Larry, Moe, and Curly Joe and another man she'd never seen before strode in.

"Oh, no," Kristie whimpered. "I've seen them here before too. I don't think they're here to apply for a job."

They walked straight for Donnie's office, not looking to the left or right.

"Wait!" Sarah called out. "I don't think—"

The tall one turned and gave Sarah such an evil glare that she felt a chill from head to toe. She couldn't move.

The man with the tattoo yanked Donnie's door open. "I knew you'd be here, Kincaid. I think we should talk."

The four men stepped inside, and the door slammed shut.

Kristie glanced to the main entrance, then back to Sarah. "There've been so many cops in and out of here lately, but there are none here now. Where's a cop when you need one?"

Sarah's hand hovered over her locket. "There just might be one here in a few minutes."

A muffled crash echoed from Donnie's office, reminding Sarah of the first time the three men showed up. This time, it sounded like more had hit the floor than just Donnie's calculator.

Sarah dropped the broom to the floor. "Get out of here. Go behind the counter and stay there. I'll be right back."

Without waiting for Kristie to move or reply, Sarah ran straight for the closet.

She saw one of the men with a gun trained on Kincaid, who was backed into the corner. Everything had been knocked off Donnie's desk, including his computer, except for the duffel bag Kincaid had just brought. The man with the tattoo and the new man held Donnie against the wall. The tall man stood inches from Donnie's face.

"I think you owe me a little money. Where is it?"

Donnie shook his head. "I don't know what you're talking about."

The man punched Donnie in the stomach. He tried to double over, but the other two men kept him upright.

Sarah thought she was going to throw up. She flicked open the locket and pressed the button.

Just in case the two presses were too far apart, she started counting to twenty.

When she got to five, the man hit Donnie again. "I don't have anything!" Donnie called out.

When she got to fifteen, the man snickered. "Maybe I'll help you remember."

He pulled a gun out of his pocket, turned, and ran out the door.

Sarah hit the button again.

Kristie screamed.

Sarah froze. She had told Kristie to get behind the counter, but she hadn't made sure Kristie actually moved.

Suddenly, the man shuffled back into Donnie's office with Kristie, his fingers entwined in her hair, and the gun pointed to her head.

"Does this make you remember?"

"Don't give it to him!" Kincaid bellowed. He was rewarded with a punch in the stomach.

Tears streamed down Kristie's face. Sarah ran out of the closet. Matt had told her that it would be about five minutes, maybe more, by the time a police officer arrived after the second push of the button. She didn't know how much time had elapsed, but she knew it wasn't much, yet already so much had happened.

She ran into the kitchen, straight for the phone, but before she reached it, footsteps echoed from the doorway.

Sarah ducked so she was below the level of the counter.

A male voice sounded from the entrance to the kitchen. "I know you're in here!"

From her position, Sarah glanced to the still-open closet door. She would never make it back to the closet without being seen.

Kristie screamed again.

Sarah's gut clenched. She had no idea how many seconds or minutes had passed since she'd pressed the button the third time.

The man crossed the room and yanked the phone off the wall. "Come on, Sarah. Where are you? You know you can't hide from me forever."

Sarah covered her mouth with her hands and forced herself to breathe. The man knew her name, although she didn't know how. She wished she could tell how much time had gone by, but she couldn't. She fumbled with the locket, pressed the button again, and did the only thing she could think of.

She began to pray.

❧

Matt stepped out of the squad car to investigate a vehicle he had pulled over for a speeding infraction when the vibration started in his hip. His gut clenched, and he ran the last few steps to the driver's window.

"Stay in the car," he said to a young male, one of many young males in the older sedan, all of whom were wearing baseball caps, on backwards. He reached to the button on his portable radio. "16Bravo4."

"16Bravo4 copy."

"There's something happening at Donnie's Donuts. Hold on a few seconds."

"Copy."

Matt counted to twenty, then counted another five. "Kincaid just walked into Donnie's Donuts. Send a plain car."

"16Bravo4 copy. ETA eight minutes."

"16Bravo4 copy."

Matt heaved a sigh of relief. He didn't like Sarah in the same building as Kincaid, but he'd told her to keep her distance. If she stayed away from trouble, trouble wouldn't go looking for her.

If she did get in trouble, he didn't know what he would do. He loved her more than life itself. He could tell she at least liked him to some degree, yet he had to know where she was at spiritually before he could deepen their relationship. At the same time, part of him didn't want to know. He was too afraid the answer wouldn't be what he needed to hear.

Yet, last night, for the first time she hadn't simply asked him t say a generic "grace." She'd specifically asked him to pray. A whil ago, she'd borrowed his Bible, then bought her own. She showe him how she'd started making her own notes. Even though the were sloppy, he had told her that he was proud of her. That ha proven what he'd heard from Dave. Sarah had been to church a least a couple of times on her own in the past month, plus she' attended every Wednesday night Bible study meeting, even whe he couldn't go. That had to mean something good.

Still, he didn't know where her heart really lay. He was to afraid that if he confronted her, like Nanci, any so-called decisio to follow Jesus would be because of him as a condition of thei relationship. Sarah had to come to the decision by herself, for he own reasons.

He had been trying to step back and let her go at her ow speed, but he couldn't do it anymore.

This current rotation finished the run that had him workin every weekend, and he could finally attend church. After the ser vice, he wanted to sit down and talk to Sarah without having t think about Donnie's Donuts and all that went with it. He had t find out where she was in her spiritual walk—then make a decisio To keep on the way he was going, loving her so deeply, yet nc knowing for sure that she shared his faith, was tearing him apart.

"Uh. . .Officer?"

Matt blinked and stared at the kid behind the wheel. "Sorry, he mumbled. He cleared his throat, stiffened, and reached towar the driver's open window. "May I see your driver's license and reg istration, please?"

Matt accepted the documents and looked over them with hi flashlight. "Have you consumed any alcohol today?"

"No, sir."

"Step out of the car, please."

Matt purposely stood too close and inhaled deeply as th young man exited the car. He didn't detect the odor of alcoho nor did he smell strong mints.

"Do you know you were exceeding the speed limit?"

Before the young man answered, another vibration began on Matt's belt.

Without waiting for an answer to his question, Matt hit the button for the portable radio. "16Bravo4. Code One to Donnie's Donuts. I'm on my way. ETA four minutes. Send at least one other car."

"16Bravo4 copy."

Another vibration started on Matt's belt. He nearly threw the young man's documentation back at him. "Consider this a warning and go straight home."

Matt ran all the way to his car, flicked on the lights and sirens, and roared off. He'd barely gone a half-dozen blocks, and the vibration started again.

Matt stomped the gas pedal all the way to the floor. He didn't know what was going on at Donnie's Donuts, but he prayed that whatever it was, he wouldn't be too late.

As he pulled into the parking lot, he hit the button for the radio. "16Bravo4 arrived at Donnie's. I'm going in." He didn't see anyone in the restaurant area at all, not even the Ronsky clan, and no staff, which was too odd. He ran to the entrance with one hand on his portable radio.

Through the glass, he could see that Donnie's door was open. He couldn't make out specifics, but he detected movement. From where he stood, he could see the entire restaurant. He didn't see anyone, or any movement, except for inside Donnie's office. "16Bravo4. Request immediate backup."

The words had barely left his mouth, when a second squad car pulled up. It was Ty. Matt nodded, and both he and Ty pulled out their guns. Matt pulled the door open as quietly as possible. They went inside, guns poised, ready and alert for the slightest movement.

Outside Donnie's door, Matt nodded to Ty. They stepped into the opening in unison. Matt aimed his gun at a man holding a clerk hostage. Ty aimed at a man who was pointing a gun at

Kincaid. He didn't see Sarah anywhere.

Matt's heart sank. He had only been expecting to see the me inside the office talking. If he had known it was a hostage situation he would have stayed outside and called for the emergency respons team and a hostage negotiator. But it was too late for that.

"Drop your weapons!" he called out.

The clerk whimpered. "Help me!" Tears streamed down her face

The man with the tattoo laughed, and Curly Joe pressed th gun into the woman's temple. She squeezed her eyes shut, an her whole face tightened. "I think you've got it backwards, cop. think you should drop your weapons."

Matt tensed. He didn't know if any more members were on th way or how long they would be. Larry, Moe, and Curly Joe kne that holding Kincaid at gunpoint was a futile threat, but holding th clerk gave them a definite advantage and a no-win situation for Mat

Ty didn't lower his gun, nor did Matt. "You have nowhere t go. More units are arriving at this very minute. You might a well give up and save us all some time."

"I don't think so. Our little friend here," he motioned his hea toward Donnie, "will be opening the safe. I'm going to get wh I came for, and then I'll be on my way with the little lady, who will let go when I'm good and ready." He moved the gun. "I' going to count to five, and if you don't put the guns down b then, I'm going to—"

"Fire! Fire!" Sarah's voice shrieked from the distance.

The fire alarm screeched above them.

Curly Joe looked up at the ceiling. "What the. . ."

In a split second, Matt lowered the gun marginally and fire hitting Curly Joe in the leg.

Curly Joe released the clerk and dropped to the ground. Ma lunged forward and grabbed the gun out of his hand.

Behind him, through the ringing in his ears from the gunsh blast and the blaring of the fire alarm above, Matt heard a scuff and the smack of a gun hitting the hard, tile floor. "Dear Go please let that be Larry's gun, and not Ty's," he muttered.

Ty's voice sounded strong and even behind him. "Put your hands on your heads, and turn around. You too, Kincaid. You have the right to remain silent. . ."

The clerk's knees buckled. She sank to the ground, covered her face with her hands, and sobbed.

The main door opened and closed. Keeping his gun trained on Curly Joe where he lay on the floor, Matt turned his head for an instant to see a man's back as he ran and disappeared into the night.

"Kristie! Kristie! Are you okay?!" Sarah burst into the room. She wrapped her arms around the clerk, even though the woman was taller than Sarah, and led her out of the room.

As she passed, their eyes met for a brief second. Sarah's voice had been shaky. Her hands were trembling. Her face completely devoid of color. Her step was uneven. But, she was the most beautiful thing Matt had ever seen. He'd never loved her more.

Just as the fire alarm went silent, more sirens sounded, this time from outside, accompanied by blue and red flashing lights.

Those lights were the next best things Matt had ever seen.

"16Bravo4 out of service at Donnie's Donuts. Send the Shift NCO, shots fired. Five in custody, possibly one suspect escaped, but everything is secure. No members or civilians hurt. Request ambulance. One suspect injured. Require Identification Section and a GIS member. Suggest you immediately round up whomever Kincaid has been buying from. Let's be the first to tell them they've lost a customer. Oh, and call the fire department. Tell them it's a false alarm."

"16Bravo4 copy. Good work."

nineteen

Instead of waiting inside her apartment, Sarah waited at the front entrance. The second she saw Matt's car pull up, she ran to the curb and slid inside.

"Do you know we haven't been to church together for five weeks?"

"Yeah. I know." He put the car into gear and drove off.

Sarah turned and studied him as he drove. The last two days had been difficult for her. The police wanted statements from both her and Kristie right away. Because of that, she was late for class on Friday morning and missed part of an important assignment. Fortunately, her professor had the time to take her into the library to go over what she'd missed. On Saturday, she'd gone to the police station with Kristie to fill out statements. Some kind of official had thanked her quietly for what she'd done and let it go at that so no one would know she'd been an informant. A lawyer had contacted all the staff on Saturday to advise them that a silent partner no one knew about owned a major percentage of the business. After a couple of weeks, barring further problems, and after the government officials and the police got everything they wanted, Donnie's Donuts would be re-opened for business under another name.

Now, on Sunday morning, she was tired but happy that life could slowly go back to normal. She could only imagine what the last two days had been like for Matt.

She cleared her throat, but her words came out barely audible. "I missed you. Have you been busy?"

"You have no idea. By the time I could leave on Friday afternoon, I'd worked nineteen hours. I got a few hours sleep, then I had to go back on Saturday for another ten hours of paperwork.

I'm not exaggerating, either. I had to do the Prosecutors Sheets for the bail hearing, fill out everything, and be interviewed for the internal investigation because there had been a shooting. An NCO has to be called whenever a shot is fired and it's not in a practice session, and there are reports for that too. You name it, there's a form to fill out for it. The arrest is easy. It's the paperwork that's the killer." He paused and gave a short, humorless laugh. "You can botch a murder, but you better make sure the paperwork is done, or else."

Nothing more was said the entire trip to church.

As they stepped through the main door, Matt grasped her hand, slipped his fingers through hers, and they walked inside together.

They joined the same group of Matt's friends as the last time they'd attended together. This time, Sarah knew most of them from the Bible study meetings and from the times she'd been to church alone. They chatted before the service as they had done on previous Sundays. A few of them looked down to their joined hands, then kept talking without missing a beat.

Matt checked his watch. "I think it's time to go sit down."

The same as before, Matt led her to the back row, to a spot where they could see the entire congregation with very little effort.

He let go of her hand as they settled into their seats.

Sarah turned to him. "I can't believe how normal this is. You busted a drug ring, you arrested five criminals, you saved Kristie from a hostage crisis, and nothing's been said. Shouldn't you be in the paper?"

Matt shrugged his shoulders. "One of the other members saw an article on page twelve of the Saturday paper. It was about two paragraphs, and he had to search for it. No names mentioned."

"But you should get a medal for this!"

People around them turned their heads to stare. Sarah ducked her head and flashed them a weak smile.

He answered barely above a whisper. "No medal, Sarah. I was just doing my job."

"You can't tell me that was a normal day."

"Certainly not. But it's still my job. The service is about to begin. We can discuss this later."

Sarah turned her attention to the reason she was there in the first place, and that was to worship God. But she couldn't help but be aware of Matt's presence beside her.

She wanted to sit beside him every Sunday, or at least every Sunday he wasn't working and protecting the average citizen from broken taillights and drug runners. More than that, she wanted to spend every day with him. She didn't want to go back to seeing him only when the donut shop reopened and he had time for a break that night. In the near future, she would graduate and become a teacher, and she wouldn't see him at all.

She reached for his hand and entwined her fingers through his, just as he'd done earlier. She wanted to be with him forever. She already knew that if she got involved with him the way she wanted, life would not be easy. Police officers around the world lived dangerous lives. The divorce rate was high, and there were other problems related to high-stress jobs.

But she couldn't live without him.

When the rest of the congregation closed their eyes to pray at the end of the worship time, Sarah prayed about her relationship with Matt. She didn't want to lose him, but she did want to do God's will, whatever that would be. If Matt didn't want to see her now that the crisis at the donut shop was over, as much as it would hurt, she had to accept that.

They sat for the rest of the service without saying a word to each other. Unlike the other times, Matt didn't write notes in either the bulletin or his Bible. He sat completely still, firmly holding her hand the entire time. When the service ended, they shuffled out of their seats and began making their way to the door.

"Matt? I forgot to get a bulletin. Can I have yours?"

He turned his head as they walked. "Why? The service is over now."

"Pastor Colin told me the dates and information about the
aptism class were in the bulletin."

Matt's eyebrows arched. "When were you talking to Pastor
olin about baptism?"

"Last week, when I was at his house."

He stopped walking, forcing Sarah to stop as well. "You were
his house? Why?"

"We were talking about stuff, and we prayed together. He
as really happy when I said I wanted to be baptized and
come a member of the church. He asked if I would teach
inday school once I became a member, but I don't think I can
r a while."

"Teach Sunday school?"

Sarah sighed. "Yes. I'd love to be able to teach the children
out Jesus. Maybe they'll be able to experience His love sooner
an I did. But I have to do more studying. I think some of the
ds know more than I do, so I have some catching up to do on
y Bible stories." She smiled ear to ear at the thought.

Matt's mouth dropped open, and he pulled her to the side of
e main entrance to the sanctuary. "I don't understand. When
d you start feeling this way? It wasn't that long ago you had no
terest in God."

"I've been doing a lot of thinking lately. As they say, I think
od's been tapping me on the shoulder for a long time. I guess I
nally decided to listen."

Before she realized what was happening, Matt's arms were
ound her. "That's wonderful," he murmured in her ear. "Praise
e Lord! It will be wonderful to see you every Sunday and
ible study meeting when I'm not working."

Hesitantly, she wrapped her arms around his back. "I want to
e you more than just Sunday mornings and Wednesday nights.
think I'm falling in love with you, and I don't know what to
. I'm scared."

Beneath her touch, Matt stiffened from head to toe. His
nds moved to her shoulders, and he slowly backed up. He

studied her face while his hands held her steadily in place
don't think I've fallen in love with you."

Sarah's heart sank. She wanted to run away. Maybe even cr

Matt's voice dropped in pitch. "I *know* I've fallen in love w
you. And I'm scared too."

Sarah sucked in a deep breath as his words sank in. !
reached forward and wrapped her hands around the sides of
waist. "You're a big strong cop. You're not supposed to
scared. Doesn't that go with the uniform?"

"Beneath the uniform, I'm just an ordinary guy." He grinn
one eyebrow raised, and his beautiful blue eyes sparkled. "Un
you're one of those chicks who only digs the uniform."

Sarah couldn't help herself. She actually giggled. "I'm ju
chick who digs the ordinary guy beneath one particular unifo
And speaking of that, you first got to know me from behind
counter at Donnie's Donuts. How do I know you're not on
those guys who only digs a woman in uniform?"

Matt snickered, then became instantly serious. "This ordin
guy wants to marry that woman, uniform or not. I know it
big decision, and you don't have to answer right away, but
like you to think about it."

Sarah's heart nearly burst. "I don't have to think about it.
answer is yes!"

Matt leaned forward, like he was about to kiss her, tl
stopped. He looked around. "Do you know this is the same pl
where we met out of uniform for the first time? While it seen
fitting spot to meet, it's probably not the best spot to prop
How about if we go somewhere else, and let me do it properly

Sarah smiled and gave his hand a squeeze. Once again, t
started walking toward the door. "Sounds like a good idea. (
anyplace in mind?"

"Yeah. Any place that doesn't sell donuts."

A Letter To Our Readers

Dear Reader:

In order that we might better contribute to your reading enjoyment, we would appreciate your taking a few minutes to respond to the following questions. We welcome your comments and read each form and letter we receive. When completed, please return to the following:

Fiction Editor
Heartsong Presents
PO Box 719
Uhrichsville, Ohio 44683

1. Did you enjoy reading *A Donut a Day* by Gail Sattler?
☐ Very much! I would like to see more books by this author!
☐ Moderately. I would have enjoyed it more if

_____

_____

_____

2. Are you a member of **Heartsong Presents**? ☐ Yes ☐ No
If no, where did you purchase this book? _____

_____

3. How would you rate, on a scale from 1 (poor) to 5 (superior), the cover design? _____

4. On a scale from 1 (poor) to 10 (superior), please rate the following elements.

____	Heroine	____	Plot
____	Hero	____	Inspirational theme
____	Setting	____	Secondary characters

5. These characters were special because?_____

_____

_____

6. How has this book inspired your life?_____

_____

_____

7. What settings would you like to see covered in future
   Heartsong Presents books? _____

_____

_____

8. What are some inspirational themes you would like to see
   treated in future books? _____

_____

_____

9. Would you be interested in reading other **Heartsong
   Presents** titles? ❏ Yes ❏ No

10. Please check your age range:

      ❏ Under 18   ❏ 18-24

      ❏ 25-34   ❏ 35-45

      ❏ 46-55   ❏ Over 55

Name_____

Occupation _____

Address _____

City_____ State_____ Zip_____

Christmas Duty

Life is never still in the military. Even Christmas is a season of challenge. . .a season of change. This year, several servicemen and women will face a range of life altering experiences.

Will these military personnel find Christmas to be a time of renewed hope? Will they hold on to their faith in the Christmas Child and the Savior who can guide their lives today?

Contemporary, paperback, 352 pages, 5 $^3/_{16}$" x 8"

♥ ♥ ♥ ♥ ♥ ♥ ♥ ♥ ♥ ♥ ♥ ♥ ♥ ♥ ♥

♥ ♥ ♥ ♥ ♥ ♥ ♥ ♥ ♥ ♥ ♥ ♥ ♥ ♥

------- Presents -------

Great Inspirational Romance at a Great Price!

Heartsong Presents books are inspirational romances in contemporary and historical settings, designed to give you an enjoyable, spirit-lifting reading experience. You can choose wonderfully written titles from some of today's best authors like Hannah Alexander, Andrea Boeshaar, Yvonne Lehman, Tracie Peterson, and many others.

When ordering quantities less than twelve, above titles are $3.25 each.
Not all titles may be available at time of order.